Zed

Zed

ROSEMARY HARRIS

A nervous eight-year-old, Thomas Z. Amsterel, goes with his admired and dreaded father to visit his uncle's office. Uncle Omar is the manager of the London branch of a Lebanese firm, and as Thomas and his father arrive they are unexpectedly caught up in a terrorist attack by the Free Army of United Arabia.

For four terrible days, an irrelevant and unwanted hostage, the small boy watches a drama of courage and cowardice, unexpected cruelty and even more unexpected kindness. The experience is devastating and begins the process of turning frightened, inadequate Thomas into clever, confident Zed. Whether that process was entirely for the better was a question he would only ask himself some years later . . .

Zed

ROSEMARY HARRIS

MAMMOTH

First published in Great Britain 1982
by Faber & Faber Limited
Magnet paperback edition published 1985
Published 1990 by Mammoth
an imprint of Mandarin Paperbacks
Michelin House, 81 Fulham Road, London SW3 6RB

Mandarin is an imprint of the Octopus Publishing Group

Copyright © 1982 Rosemary Harris

ISBN 0 7497 0529 9

A CIP catalogue record for this title
is available from the British Library

Printed in Great Britain
by Cox & Wyman Ltd, Reading, Berkshire

1 IT WAS ALL MacArthur's idea. He sent for me late, after games practice was over, and I went along to the staff room wishing he'd kept whatever it was for tomorrow. It had been a strenuous day, from early physics to late afternoon mud and battle out at Twickenham, and I felt the school owed me a rest.

The nervous junior who brought the message had been hanging round the entrance when our school bus drew in. "Mr. MacArthur wants to see Thomas Amsterel at once, before he goes home," he announced, and stared at me pop-eyed before he fled, as though I'd been caught with my hand on the Headmaster's silver. It was unlike MacArthur to be urgent about small things, and my gloom increased.

He looked relaxed enough when I got there: feet up on the table, in a way you don't expect from your house master, coffee and some papers by his side.

"Ah, come in, Zed," he greeted me, peering at me over his spectacles and ignoring the fact that I was in already. "I thought that I should add my own congratulations on your exam results."

It did just cross my mind that he could have done so any time during the day. And not when I was dying for tea.

"Thanks, it was nothing." I saw the slight twist to the smile, and added rather fast: "Actually, I was pretty relieved."

"And what do you plan to do now?"

I was floored. You can imagine. Pause to breathe was the obvious answer, but I didn't quite say so, in spite of those feet on the table, and the coffee. I looked away from him, out of the window, into the gardens at the back of the school. The chestnuts were curly with bright green buds in spite of London dirt, and there were splodges of mauve and orange crocus, and sparrows picking at them. There was a flowering tree, too, dropping red petals. That tree always reminds me of another . . .

The school cat was creeping towards the sparrows, belly-flat. Without thinking, I made a loud spitting noise.

"*What?*" MacArthur sounded thunderous.

"Sorry, sir. It's that cat again. It's a thug, it's after the sparrows, and then it goes for the blackbirds. There won't be a bird left, soon—" I warmed to my theme, hoping to turn his thoughts to my zeal for ecology.

He took his feet off the table then, and stood up. He's a hugely tall man, and he towered over me.

"You're very self-confident, Zed; in general, you cope very well."

He paused, giving me time to feel embarrassed. MacArthur has such good timing, he should have been an actor.

"There's your pocket size, for one thing," he went on. "You're like greased lightning out there on the field. Admirable, that goal you scored against Melbourne's last week. Not that the side isn't a strong one, still—"

All pure butter—except for that reference to my size. MacArthur smiled at me rather grimly, and poured out more coffee and pushed it across to me.

"Seeing that you've done so well for yourself, Zed—even if some of it's façade—and seeing that you're at a bit of a loose end, and it happens to be our school centenary this summer, I thought you might care to occupy yourself with doing something for us, before the end of this term?"

I was instantly on my guard. "At a loose end"? I hadn't noticed anyone lying about in hammocks, not even now the pressure of O levels was over and done with. It seemed to me there was never extra time for anything—so I muttered something pathetic which implied the whole school was leaning its weight on me already.

MacArthur paid no attention. He was staring down reflectively on those papers by his side.

"Come and glance at these, will you." He gave me one of his famous X-ray looks. Careful, I told myself, as I moved round the table to join him, he's up to something. Even so, I wasn't prepared to see that black familiar headline again, splashed across yellowing paper. My whole inside did a somersault as it hadn't since I was eight. Eight and two weeks and two days, to be exact. And two hours and a quarter. I counted it all up at the time, like counting sheep, on one of those bad four nights, and that sort of detail sticks for ever.

"Funny—" MacArthur was saying—"but I never knew you were that child."

There was a quietness between us. You could almost have heard the dust settle. Streams of late sunlight were coming in through the window grittily, full of motes. The room seemed very big and hollow—and I felt very small again, small as an eight-year-old, and the boom of traffic blazing past on the road beyond the square came in waves, loud on the warmish air. It was an odd feeling, as though time had stopped altogether seven years back—but that paper was yellow, so it hadn't.

There was a new colour supplement beside the old newspaper. It was yesterday's, and belonged to a paper my family didn't take. MacArthur was opening it at a full central spread. I leaned forward to see, my hands gripping the table edge. There was another black banner of a headline: "Where are they today?" and beneath that were photographs with captions in smaller type.

It seemed to be a typical sort of special feature. The left-hand page carried two pictures of a German girl who'd done time for bank robbery in Frankfurt, "Today a model housewife", and some Yank who passed secret papers to Moscow,

"Now working with destitute children in South America". The girl was shown raising a gun, then wielding a duster. The man first scowling in custody, later conducting an orphans' choir. But it was the bottom half of the right-hand page that held my startled attention: a large rectangular colour print of a family group.

The boy must have been about twelve years old. He was standing beside a stoutish middle-aged man whose right hand rested heavily on his shoulder—it looked rather a warder-to-prisoner touch. On his other side stood a slight woman in black, with a narrow sad-looking face and huge dark eyes. The caption read: "This is Noora Fatima—now married to an Arabian diplomat stationed in London, whose one time first husband—see oval insert—" I didn't finish reading, I knew already what it would say.

I stared at the oval. It was obviously an amateur snap, a bit blurry. In spite of that, and though the printed name beneath it was strange to me, I knew him at once. The proud lift to his head, the thinnish face, the dark yet amused look, the prominent nose. The boy in the other picture would be his son, Feisal, who was three years younger than me. The likeness between them was too strong to be missed. Feisal was staring straight into camera, and I thought: he looks unhappy, he's appealing to me, perhaps he doesn't like his stepfather. And then: help! I must be crazy. I bent my head and read through twice, very carefully, what was written beneath the picture. It gave me time to recover.

So I hardly heard MacArthur rabbiting on beside me, till I caught up at—

"—of course it must have been before my appointment here, I'm forgetting. And you'd have been in the Junior School. And later on, when you moved up...no, I heard nothing about it then."

"You were away, sir, that term I moved up from Albert's," I mumbled. Prince Albert's is our own Junior School which prepares you for the main school, Prince Consort's—if anything could. It's almost next door and takes only day pupils—spotty little apes that we do our best to ignore. Consort's takes both boarders and day boys. I'm a day, and prefer it, but I've sometimes had spells of boarding when my mixed bag of a family has been in the States, or the Middle East. It seems a long while since I was a Junior myself, though MacArthur's proddings around in my past brought it all back to me.

"Ah yes—you moved up in my sabbatical," MacArthur was saying. "So you weren't in any of my classes till the following spring . . . and there are so many things to keep track of in a school year, aren't there, Zed?"

He was watching me now, waiting for me to say something, so I asked him resentfully, "Who kept that old paper?"

He shook his head. "It was there in the library, with other cuttings for that year. We've been going through all the old files, the Headmaster and I, to see what might be of interest for the school magazine's Centenary Number."

I winced at the thought of our new Headmaster seeing that paper. He was appointed only last term, and we were still trying to sum him up.

MacArthur was looking at me expectantly, and I couldn't guess at his thoughts. I looked away—at the crocuses' upside-down arrowheads—and immediately saw them sticking up mauve and orange in the windowboxes seven years ago, that fine morning we walked up Regency Gate together, my father and I. And I thought of 'Arabi' too, as I often did. The man in the photograph. Whose real name I'd never known.

"—it would be something special for the Centenary Number," MacArthur was saying. "So far it's an indifferent collection. I suppose we could always fill up with school photographs, but—dull. So how would it be if you wrote it all up for us? Your experience. Your own words. How it all seemed to you at the time? What it did—or didn't—do for you."

I was still staring at the crocuses. And the cat, lying in shadow, thin, black and disturbing. I didn't say anything. I was remembering reporters lying in wait like that cat; the policeman guarding the main door of our block of flats; my mother, angry-eyed and tightlipped, taking off the telephone receiver; and the way everyone we met seemed to want something of us—to hold us or touch us in some way, curious, friendly, greedy, demanding. The silence stretched on and on. I felt very tired suddenly. All the good feeling and pleasure I'd felt on the playing field had drained right out of me. I had a fancy it was lying in puddles round my feet, if you could see it.

"Sorry, sir?"

"I said it was very much an event of our time, yet very tough for a child of your age—eight, weren't you? An adult doesn't often come through such a gruelling experience unscathed. I must admit, Zed, I'm curious about you! I've looked up your earliest records, and you seem to have struck your first teachers as a timid, uncertain child. Perhaps rather crushed at home—um? So I feel what you might contribute from your—well—special viewpoint, could be valuable. Will you have a stab at it? You write me an excellent essay —when you try."

I was going to refuse. Definitely. Not even MacArthur could make me, if I didn't want to—and I certainly didn't. Not for the school—not for the Centenary Number that would be passed round all the parents too. Not for the Headmaster to beam sunnily and congratulate me on 'having found my identity'—something he was fond of urging on us, like a treasure hunt. Not for anyone. It was my private thing, and I looked at the red-flowering tree and thought about Arabi again.

"Well, I'm sorry, Zed." MacArthur's voice sounded really regretful, as though he were speaking to an adult. "You must forgive me—I can see that I've made a mistake. Forget it."

That's the sort of thing which makes us like him so much
—and also makes me wonder sometimes if he's a bit of a
bastard. Because of course I turned round then and said that
I'd do it, before I'd even time to think about it twice.

2 So THERE I was, stuck with it. By way of bait MacArthur offered me any number of music tapes to get me in the mood, half an hour off work at the end of each day, and the use of an empty study at the back of the school. There I sat after teatime, biting my pen, watching the sunlight on the grass, and cursing myself. Why hadn't I stuck to refusal? I knew the anwer, of course: MacArthur, with his pleasant form of friendly cunning, had caught me off guard.

The paper was too white, too empty. I wrote my name on the top page: Thomas Z. Amsterel, and sat back gloomily looking at it. Fine, so far as it went. Nice large black letters, reminding me of those headlines, but making the paper round them look whiter and emptier still. After a while I drew some elephants in striped pants playing soccer, and a crude sketch of MacArthur as referee with the words: "Goal! Keep coping, Zed," coming out of his mouth on a balloon. Then I threw the page into the wastepaper basket, played through an old Brubeck tape, and gave up for the day.

All that week, it was no good. Time after time I got out of class early and sat down in the study, gazed at the paper, and played through MacArthur's tapes. The school cat got thinner, and the sparrows craftier—they must have MacArthur blood.

At last I worked out one paragraph. Not bad words, but empty. They hadn't caught anything real. For the first time it dawned on me that writing an essay and being a writer are two completely different things—and I wasn't a writer. Then and there I decided to tell MacArthur that I simply couldn't do it. He hadn't been seen that day, so I went along to the staff room. He wasn't there, either—only George Shirley, who teaches us French lang. and lit. with a ripe Midlands accent.

"Have you seen Mr. MacArthur?" I asked. I was getting so desperate that I added, "Please?"

He shut his book with a bang, shaking his head. "He has this unpleasant spring bug—'flu, or whatever it is. His wife says he won't be teaching next week, either." He looked at me closely. "Something wrong, Zed? Can I help?"

I told him in a rather muddled way, and he looked worried. And annoyed.

"Hell, this would happen! He asked me to make sure that number's getting into shape—and a whole section is being kept for you. Can't you have another shot at it?"

"I suppose so." I felt close to tears. I haven't cried since I was eight, and I hoped he wouldn't notice. But Shirley's X-ray glance is second only to MacArthur's.

"You might try the madeleine approach. Proust's," he suggested drily.

"Madeleine Proust?" I said blankly.

He rocked himself back on his heels. "*Marcel* Proust, Zed —upon whose writings we have had no fewer than three sessions last term, if I may remind you. I assume you were paying attention at the time?"

You can't tell masters that it's never safe to assume anything. In fact I'd been coasting in Shirley's lessons, giving my mind a well-earned rest. However—I dug around in it and delved up a faint picture of this Proust chewing away at some French bun or biscuit called a madeleine, and finding the smell and flavour triggered off a niagara of memory, which caused him to sit down and write at least a dozen boring volumes which, in my view, the world could well have done without.

"Oh, *that* Proust. I see what you mean, sir. But it's not exactly my problem, it's more—"

He wasn't listening. "Anything that could help you in that

line? Let it all out, boy, and then select, select. Er—tea? Coke?"

I could see he was trying to be human.

"Maybe chocolate," I said, after a moment's thought "Very black warm sticky chocolate."

And I felt that crazy urge to cry again.

Shirley shambled to his feet, looking relieved, and fumbled in the table drawer. "Ah—well—I wonder what we have— Hah!" He pounced on a bar of something wrapped in torn silver paper. "See what you can do on that, Zed. It's certainly dark, and I've no doubt you can make it warm and sticky."

"Thank you, sir."

"And though you're not writing a book, you could think of it as such, and cut it down later."

I was just beginning to think he was almost on MacArthur's level, when he added: "Oh—and Zed. Once you've finished, you might just write me three or four pages on what you know of Marcel Proust. In French, if you please. You speak it fluently enough, but your written work is atrocious."

Masters! I thought, as I plodded back to my study. And I hadn't even got it across to Shirley that my memory was all right—or most of it. How would these fossilized masters like to try thinking themselves back into an eight-year-old's skin?

Shut into that empty room again, I tried to empty myself too: get rid of older Zed. I put the chocolate on the desk and stared at it, then unwrapped it and licked it lingeringly. The flavour was nuttier, the bar a lighter colour than the squares Arabi had given me. His had been kept in his shirt pocket, and the warmth of his body had begun to melt it and make it sticky. I could almost taste that chocolate again now . . . see that cold room with its rigged-up light. Feel a stifling sense of loss and fear.

Shirley's scheme was a terrible one. And I couldn't begin with Day Four of the nightmare. I felt sick right through at the idea . . . sicker than on the first morning of the whole

16

four-day stretch, when I was walking up Regency Gate with my father.

Suddenly I thought: maybe that's where I should begin, my hand held tight in his, stumbling along trying to keep up with his powerful, impatient strides? And: yes, I can almost feel myself eight years old again—as though the past has come alive inside me, and it's all happening now. What was it Shirley had said? "Let it all out, boy, and then select, select."

I half closed my eyes, let my mind drift where it wanted to, and began to write.

3   THE PALM OF my hand was warm and sticky, and my
     father's hand was large and cold and gripped mine
     uncomfortably hard. I had to jog to keep up with
him, but the more I jogged the hotter I grew, and my breakfast egg seemed to have stuck halfway down. It was the egg
that made me feel sick, perhaps—though I might have felt all
right if I'd been with Uncle Omar. Or with Christl, who
helped my mother about the flat. The pavements ahead
looked very broad, and the streets broader still. It was an
uphill jog. The park was green at the top of Regency Gate,
and still looked a long way off.

"Didn't you wash after breakfast?" My father's voice was
far above my head.

Jog, jog. I couldn't anwer, in case the egg came up.

We reached a crossing, and had to wait. I drew a deep
breath, just held back the egg, and blurted out an unconvinc-
ing "Yes."

"Don't lie—your hand's disgusting, Thomas." He
dropped it. I waited beside him, gazing at the traffic with
swimming eyes, and wished I was back in our sunny flat,
watching Sheikhah give my cousin Ali Baha his breakfast
—he'd taken to English breakfasts in a big way. She was so
nice and round and funny, my Aunt Sheikhah. Baha loved
egg, and when she cracked the top for him his pink lips curled
up, moist with pleasure, and he beamed so that his fat cheeks
almost swallowed his black eyes.

Baha was nearly five, and a fine big boy for his age, my
mother said. Even my father seemed to like him, although he
called him "that Saudi brat" behind Aunt Sheikhah's back.

18

I'd got used to people admiring Baha, and I didn't hold it against him, for I loved him too. I just wished that I could change places with him, that was all, and not be "our little fruit cocktail", as my father sometimes called me. There's a lot of fruit grown in the part of Lebanon where my mother comes from. I hadn't been there since I was Baha's age, and I just had hazy memories of it. My grandfather, holding me up in his arms to pull ripe mulberries from the tree. Their squashy inky purple as I crammed them into my mouth. Being put to rest in the shade while a ripple of Arabic or French ran on above my head. Being smacked for pulling blooms off my grandmother's flowers. That sort of thing.

Baha was never smacked. He'd been naughty that morning, thwacking his little derbakki drum wildly all round the breakfast table, his cheeks bright pink with pleasure, and he thwacked louder still when Uncle Omar said he was to stop. All the same, Omar merely picked him up and kissed him goodbye, smackingly, on either cheek, and Baha flung his arms round his neck and kissed him back with an equally smacking and eggier kiss. There was a very good feeling between them.

"You've got a fine son there," my father said, sighing.

"So have you," Uncle Omar had replied, touching my shoulder as he passed me on his way out. He wasn't a large, impressive man like my Anglo-American father, he was thin and wiry, with the same huge black eyes as Ali Baha, and a drooping black moustache. *He* was some sort of cocktail too, I suppose, since his father was a Saudi and his mother Turkish. It seems the Saudis were still very poor when Uncle Omar's father was young, there was no money anywhere, it was before the oil boom. So he'd left the desert and gone to work in Lebanon for a rich Turkish merchant, and ended by marrying the old man's only daughter.

My Uncle Omar was their favourite, cleverest son. He was a Muslim, of course, so his marriage to my mother's younger sister had made a scandal—because her family were Maronites. It was my mother who often talked to me about our family background, and I was secretly as proud of it as she was, and fascinated by the ancient feuds and loyalties stretching back, back into the past, to the seventh century.

Sometimes, when she was in a good mood, my mother would tell me stories of the old persecutions, before our Christian sect fled up into the mountain high above the sea, to escape their Byzantine and Muslim enemies. The mountains were a strong shield and refuge for minorities, she told me, and our Christian sect was strong among them. Up in the crystal mountains—the Christian Mountain, my mother called it—they grew arrogant, rich and powerful, a force to be reckoned with throughout the Lebanon. "We are the only true Lebanese, Thomas, and your grandfather is an important man among them—and a very powerful Sheikh."

"But why were we called Maronites?" I ventured once.

"Oh, because we first came to the teaching of a saint—St. Maron he was—in Antioch. That's why our Patriarch is Patriarch of Antioch and all the East," she told me proudly.

"And a hotly disputed title it is, five times over," chipped in my father mockingly. He was irritated by my interest, and specially bored by the Christian-Muslim feuding between my mother's family and Uncle Omar's. All he'd say scoffingly was that the least said about that scrap between two packs of quarrelsome fanatical Arabs, the better.

Again, it was my mother who explained about it, shortly before Aunt Sheikhah and Ali Baha arrived in England to stay with us, three months ahead of Uncle Omar, who was coming to take up the post of Managing Director at his grandfather's offices in London.

"Both sides fumed," said my mother in her pretty French, pouting at herself in the mirror. "You can imagine it, my little one! My marrying your father was bad enough—oh, the lamenting! An Englishman, with an American half-Jewish mother! But at least he was Catholic (poor Corney, who only goes to Mass twice a year, but they didn't know *that*). *I* was almost disowned, do you see?" She tossed her thick black curls, watching herself in the dressing table glass, then sprayed herself heavily with scent. Her laugh tinkled, her gold bracelets clashed. "Yola—*she* was quite disowned. A Muslim! She had to run away to marry him, and she hasn't been home since. Imagine that."

She sprayed herself again, and I sneezed, spotting her shirt with moisture. Seeing her frown, I asked hurriedly, "Where did they marry?" This tale of Yola was romantic, like a story. I loved hearing about my Arab relatives, though my father seemed determined to discount them.

As though thinking of him too she switched suddenly to English. "Where else but Cyprus? They couldn't marry in the Lebanon—both families were furious, and anyhow a Muslim and a Christian *cannot* marry there. Of course his family won't forgive her, ever—even though they forgave him soon enough. It's always the same, men get away with anything. Don't touch that nail varnish." She began to paint her nails, jabbing at them with the brush, expert little scarlet streaks. I risked another question.

"Why isn't she called Yola still?"

"Why indeed? Because she became a Muslim. Why should the woman change her faith, and not the man?" She shot me a furious glance under her long lashes. I couldn't help it if I was going to be a man, and it was such a long way off anyway.

"I hope I shall remember that my own little sister Yola has turned into Sheikhah—and a doormat," she was saying. Her eyes went flash, flash. "At least she could have stopped Omar giving Baha those appalling names."

"Why?" I asked timidly. Muhammad Ali Baha seemed to me a nice name, much nicer than Thomas Zachary, and part of it would turn easily into Alley Bear, which could be an even better nickname.

"Muhammad Ali after their Prophet and his son-in-law, and Baha after the biographer of Sala-ud-din! He just did it to annoy our family and show them who's master now—I tell you, he's part Turk, and they haven't altered." At that time I had only the vaguest idea of who or what Muhammad and Saladin were; but when my mother scowled like that, and began popping and unpopping the press studs in her shirt, I knew better than to ask more questions.

Her wet nails were smearing varnish on her shirt, but she hadn't noticed. "Only an arrogant Turk would expect me to put up his wife and child while he went jetting round the world on business. Or a Saudi, they're as bad," she added, "and they all think women should be kept hidden away in paper bags. Don't you dare speak Arabic too much when they get here, you'll annoy your father, and—What are you staring at?" She saw the varnish. "Oh! Why didn't you tell me, Thomas, you little pig?" She smacked my face.

I left the room in tears. She often took it out on me when she longed to row with someone else.

My Uncle Omar, when he did arrive at last, proved to be both kind and gentle. Still, there was something about him, some hint of past desert pride or distant Turkish warrior, which made even my mother act differently in his presence, although he was only a business man and an international lawyer, small and merry, whose wife cocooned herself in gauzy scarves, never, ever, argued with her husband—and even dared tell my mother that Muhammad Ali Baha's name was their own business.

But there was another reason, I learned later, why my mother was so annoyed about his naming: it reminded her of my own father's highhandedness over second name.

"Zachary!" She spat it at him like a little cat, one day when Sheikhah had gone out. "As bad as Ali Baha! How could you ever shame me like that, Corney? Why should my poor father have two sons-in-law who long only to insult him?" I thought she looked and sounded like someone in our school play.

"Insult him? Why—how could I do that, Leila?" My father was play-acting too. He wore a familiar smile.

"We have enough trouble from the Israelis, without your calling my own son by a Jewish name."

"Yours? Our little fruit cocktail is a fair mix of nations. Come here, my Thomas Zachary—" I obeyed and, planting me between his knees, my father held me there, and looked me over. I was sure he didn't mean to be unkind, he looked so noble, with his wide forehead and fair hair. My mother was watching him half resentfully, half adoring. It surely wasn't his fault that I was no use for anything.

"Where does your Jewish-American grandmother come out, I wonder? Not in that blob of nose—" he tweaked it. "Anyway—" he spoke over my head, still holding me— "respect my mother's memory, please, Leila. She was a very shrewd woman, much of our security comes from her. As for this Middle East problem in miniature—" he rumpled my hair and laughed—"he'll be as English a cocktail as they can shake him into at Prince Albert's. How have you liked your time there, Thomas? Shall we be proud of you, in the end?"

My eyes filled with tears, as they so easily did. I hadn't liked it at all.

His hands released me. "Oh—go and play with Alley Bear."

My hand on the doorknob, I looked back. They'd forgotten me already; they were gazing at each other—I knew that soft, funny look they both wore sometimes, when all the temper left my mother's face, and her eyes grew larger still and swimmy. She was getting fatter all the time just then, like a fat sleepy pear. She said she was getting me a brother or sister, I wasn't quite sure how. People always said "your lovely mother", but noses and mouths and eyes didn't mean lovely, to me. Only how people were with you. Most people said Aunt Sheikhah was plain, but I didn't know what that meant, either. She was kind to everyone, even me, but of course she put Alley Bear and Uncle Omar first.

It may have been having so many relatives to stay that made my parents specially cross just then. Or the bad news in the papers, that always seemed to be about the Lebanon, or the Palestinians and Israel, and people shooting. Anyway. the sniping had crept into our family circle. Some of it was due to my mother's refusal to entertain someone called Mr. Mizerachi in her home. "Whatever that Israeli's here for, we do not have to ask him to our flat."

"Very well, Leila," said my father, yielding at last, "but I can't let emotion interfere with business. Perhaps Omar could arrange a meeting for us, one of these days."

"Christl," I asked later, "who's Mr. Mizerachi?"

"Thomas—always questions! I cannot tell you more than you already know, *Kind*. Your uncle and your father seem to think he's an important man—and his photograph was in last Sunday's paper."

She brought it and showed it to me. It wasn't a good snap: a man in a black hat, hurrying along in streaming rain.

"He looks just like anyone," I said, rather disappointed. It seemed silly that someone like that could have caused so much rowing.

My school term had just ended, and my mother kept trying to tease my father to take the three of us home to see her family, while he growled darkly about not speaking French or Arabic. He didn't really like my being good at either language, I knew that. It was another form of failure that I didn't understand.

"I don't suppose Thomas wants to spend his holidays out there, do you, Thomas?"

I was in two minds about it. I liked the thought of sea and mountains, of running in the orchards, of hot drowsy mealtimes in the sun when my grandfather, with his huge turned-up moustaches and enormous laugh, fed me with black bean *fool*, or *baklava* stuffed with almond and pistachio and oozing syrup. I didn't like the thought of flying, or the grandmother who smacked me and told my grandfather: "Don't give that child more Lady's Navel, Maroun—he'll be sick." Lady's Navel oozed even more syrup than *baklava*, it was my sweetest memory in every way.

"I'm not sure," I said, anxious to please both sides.

"It might even be a treat to get away from such close quarters with that damn Saudi and his brat—give that family time to find a flat of their own. I'm not making our travel arrangements, though—and my secretary's got enough to do." My father does public relations for a big oil company: that was how he came to meet my mother—travelling in the Middle East.

"Of course not, Corney." Her voice sounded sweet as *baklava*, now she had her way. "Omar will arrange it all, their business owns a charter flight company—trust them! And he tells me the office is on the ground floor, just beneath his own. Yola—Sheikhah would like him to do something for us, so would he."

"All right, then. We'll leave everything to him." My father was cheering up. "You take Thomas to your family, and I'll arrange some time off and combine it with burnishing my company's image in Beirut, my bosses will approve of that." She gave him a sharp glance, and he added casually, "Tell Omar I don't mind picking up the tickets and flight details once he's fixed them—he can give me lunch one day. I'm told they do themselves extremely well with their expenses."

Three days later Uncle Omar told us over breakfast that everything should be ready. "If you look in later this morning, Cornelius, the girl downstairs will have everything you want. Then come on upstairs to me, I'm on the first floor. Come at twelve-thirty—that's a good plan: if Mizerachi can be available we'll all go out and lunch together."

Omar's English was very good; of course it had to be. And

25

in front of my father he never spoke Arabic. "Why don't you bring Thomas, too?" he added. "You're both on holiday, and we could give him a beautiful ice-cream—orange, straw-berry, black cherry?"

I knew he was being kind, but I wanted to stay home with Aunt Sheikhah and Alley Bear. He had that new derbakki drum, and I was teaching him how to tap it, now soft, now loud, till the taut skin rang excitingly, "poumpoum, poum-poumpoum."

"Yes, Thomas would like that," declared my mother. "Thank you, Omar, that's extremely kind of you." When she spoke that way even my father gave in to her. He and I would be spending hours and hours of the day together. I saw the look he gave her, and that was the moment when my egg began to stick in my throat.

4 JOG, JOG – WE were crossing the road, my father's hand on my shoulder. He had to lean down and sideways to do it, I was so small. I looked up at him, and knew I could never grow into anything so big and tough and splendid and confident, like a great blonde animal. It was just something that could never happen, except in dreams. The knowledge hurt me every day, and I went to bed with it at night. Neither prayers nor daydreams could make it happen, and there seemed no other use for me at all.

We reached a traffic island. A group of adults and children were trooping towards us. Large, bright children—they ran ahead laughing, jostling each other on to the island. They pushed me and giggled, grinning sideways. Like dogs grin, showing their teeth. I shrank away, almost beneath a car. The driver hooted at me.

"You shouldn't cower like that," my father said as we reached the farther side of the road. "Stand up to people, Thomas, they won't respect you unless you do." I looked back at the noisy group. Most children seemed to be well inside their families and trying to get out, while I was always outside, trying to get in.

"Hope this girl of Omar's hasn't lost our passports, that would finish it," said my father. "People are so stupid, these days—and my firm has the devil of a job getting visas."

"What's a visa?" I asked timidly, hoping it was a good question, the sort he liked. And I listened very hard to the answer—I mustn't ask the same thing twice. Sometimes this made me so nervous that I couldn't grasp what he said.

"A bit of paper that lets us into their damned country."

"It's our country too, though, isn't it?"

"Your mother's."

"And Aunt Sheikhah's and Uncle Omar's," I persisted unwisely, "and Alley Bear's?"

Silence. But it *was* Bear country. Half mine too, anyway, whatever my father thought. I had a nice warm feeling inside when I remembered that—and how I sat on my grandfather's knees as his car breasted the zig-zag mountain road, and he wound down the window for me to sniff the heady air, flowery, pine-y, full of juniper and sun with a good strong underlying smell of goat...

A tug on my hand. "At least we're not going to that damned Saudi's original desert dusthole. All that fuss about drinking behind closed doors with a set of undersized Arabs. Nothing to see except a lot of shapeless women bundled in black bags. Some holiday that would be."

He glanced down at me, and I wondered suddenly how he saw my mother. At least she was a big fat Arab, and getting fatter still with my mysterious brother, every day. I put up an anguished prayer to whatever cruel god had made me so small that the baby would be a tiny little girl instead. Better still, dead. Then I felt so wicked that I knew it was bound to be a strapping boy.

A tear trickled down my nose. I wiped my eyes with the back of my hand, and tripped over the edge of a paving stone.

"Thomas, can't you even look where you're going?"

My hand was gripped again, and my father fairly raced me across the last few yards to the top of Regency Gate. My egg came up in the middle of the pavement. In a way it was such relief to be rid of it that I didn't even mind the shame. And now at last there would be room for that ice-cream. It was a good light feeling, something was going to come up to expectation at last, even if it wasn't me.

Uncle Omar's company offices were on the opposite corner of the road, overlooking the park. I took deep breaths from what was now a pleasant hollow ready to be filled. Everything was suddenly brighter. I can still see the details of that scene as we approached the grand newish building, with its square green and black marble pillars, the company's name in big letters above the portico, and the security guard standing beneath, with his black holster and green uniform. The park trees were bright, bright green too, as though someone had just washed them, the buses were scarlet as a signal.

Two Japanese tourists were crossing the road behind us, from a big coach parked by the kerb. They had tiny slips of cameras, which they used sharp and sudden, like guns, snap, snap: shooting from eye-level with the speed and neatness of cowboys in my favourite old spaghetti westerns.

From the corner of my eye I saw some other people emerging from behind the stationary coach. There was a constant flutter and rush of movement, and I clung tight to my father's cold hard hand, in case I got lost among all the legs. Just outside the company entrance was a semi-circle of pink pavement, the pinkish-red dust well stamped down. I scuffed my feet through and made the dust fly, and my father said, "*Thomas*", pushing me ahead of him. I looked back, and saw the Japanese had gone on to the park, but the other people were coming up behind us, bunched together. The security guard spoke to my father, asking our names and who we wanted to see. Suddenly I felt a violent shove, and was swept forward over the threshold, still clinging to my father's hand.

"*What the hell*—" he shouted, turning round so that I turned too, swung in a semicircle from right to left.

I'm still confused about what happened next—but I saw the guard's hand at his holster. There was a loud report, and another. A stone chip hit me on the ear with a waspish sting. I yelped. The pillar beside me was pockmarked with grey-green holes. But the guard hadn't drawn his gun, he was bent over, both hands clasping his waist. He slid to the ground, lost in a tangle of that group of thrusting tourists. He was picked up, screaming, and swung against our legs, so that we were forced back into the hall. There was more pushing and jostling, and something black pressed into my father's ribs. He didn't say a word, he just let go of me. Someone slammed the great door shut, and stood against it holding a hard lemon-shaped object in one hand, finger through a crooked pin.

Next, I remember being hustled into an office on the left. People already there were screaming, one trying to open a window and failing because it stuck. My father said, loud and clear, "How dare you? We are British nationals," and was answered by a thin dark man, with a striped cloth muffling his head and face—an Arab kuffieh—who stuck the gun back in his ribs, saying very guttural and rather shaky, "You— keep quiet."

"Is it for a film, Fa—*Fa*?" I gasped. But my father paid me no attention, and a woman with long brown hair began to scream, on and on, "Oh, oh, oh", her mouth wide open, like mine when the egg came up. It was only sounds that came out, though, and those stopped when someone slapped her roughly, first on one cheek, then the other.

Another man came up to us. He was wearing a white scarf wrapped over his head and around the lower part of his face, but it had slipped sideways; beneath small black eyes like little chips of coal and a spread-looking nose showed a gleaming black moustache, so large and heavy that it seemed to have a fierce expression all its own. Beads of sweat were running down his pockmarked face. He told the first gunman, "Up-stairs—fast. Where we planned." He had a gun too, and he was plainly in command. I understood him all right, although his Arabic was so unlike my mother's.

"There's a child here—"

"*Fast.*"

We were hustled from the room and upstairs, bunched like sheep, stumbling as we ran. There were several gunmen

30

prodding us along. Climbing unsteadily, I looked down between the balusters into the hall, and saw a stain of red where the guard lay making strange grunting sounds. So it wasn't a film, it was for real—and I was already several steps behind my father, who was being shoved along, ahead of everyone. I began to cry, soundlessly. Tears half blinded me, I missed a tread and fell, banging my nose on the step next above.

A wiry arm scooped me up from behind, to carry me on up the flight. I blinked, clearing the tears, and found it was one of the gunmen who held me hard against his chest. His gun was so close to my eyes that I could see every detail—and the hand moulded to it with a grip tense and hard, brown-skinned, shiny where the knuckles caught the light.

His face was closer to me than the gun. He made a clicking sound in my ear, "Tsck!" I looked up and he was smiling, a wild, reckless smile, which had a kind of stretched look, like the skin of Alley Bear's drum set too tight. His neck muscles stood out, ropy, and in the hollows pulses were beating very quick.

He's scared too, I thought, in wonder. My tears stopped.

"That's better," he said. "You're not hurt, are you?"

I shook my head. All the time we were mounting the long curving flight, and all the time the gunbarrel, shiny blue under the lights of this high hall chandelier, covered the retreating backs ahead. I looked from the tautly smiling face above me to the gun, and down into the hall again, at the green-uniformed figure writhing on the floor. Another gunman, in blue trousers and a long flapping shirt, was bending over it.

On the landing there was more confusion, till someone's gruff command shook a pattern from it. Three men went running up the next flight, one raising his arm to shoot into the air. Plaster fell from the ceiling. Faces peering down over the circular rail above were pale and frozen, arms rose stiffly like sticks. People looked out of rooms on our floor, and were

31

jostled back into them again. I thought of Uncle Omar, couldn't see him.

The women were sorted from the men. One woman clung to her husband's hand and was dragged away, sobbing. My father just stood there, head down. He wasn't looking at me. He wasn't looking at anything.

I said, "Fa—Fa!" loudly, and wriggled. My captor put me down, and I started across the landing. The black-moustached man's guttural Arabic said, "Put him in with the women."

"*No*," I started screaming, while two strong hands seized me by the shoulders and, struggling, I found myself pushed in among woman-stuffs and woman-smells. A whirlpool of plump arms, bulging carriers, cardigans, jeans, high heels, swept me about and into itself and through a doorway across a shiny wooden floor. An armed man strode to the window, and banged the heavy shutters to, leaving only one long slit of light between them. Then, in Arabic and broken English, the women were told to move desk and chairs against the wall. There was quiet in the room now, except for gulps and sniffings. My own gulps were louder, though I tried to stop them as I craned to hear what was happening outside. Our door was still open; downstairs in the hall someone was telephoning. We were too far off to hear what was being said, even if other sounds hadn't made it impossible: protests, a jabber of snarling replies.

Sudden squeaks and chatter started up in our room again, broken with stabbing harshness by one word: "Silence!"

It was Black Moustache. And this time it was a sub-machine gun's muzzle we were looking down. He didn't have to speak again. One fat woman's whole body was wobbling, right outside her control. My legs felt all funny too, just as they had when Alley Bear's special bath toy was discovered hidden in my bed. My mouth was so dry I couldn't swallow.

My memory goes funny here, as well. Perhaps it was the

speed and shock of everything, but there's an unfillable gap till I remember myself sitting on a wooden chair against the wall where the women sat or stood in line, since there weren't enough chairs for everyone. Without really wanting to I was holding the hand of a young woman wearing jeans and purple shoes. The sub-machine gun was on the huge black desk, its muzzle slanting out between the shutters. One gunman stood behind it. Another, face entirely muffled except for his eyes, was just outside our door. And what I now think of as Day One of our captivity by a group calling itself the Free Army of United Arabia had begun.

5 AT FIRST IT was all fear and boredom. Time dragging on and on, nothing happening, just threat of guns. And cramp in my bottom, from sitting on the hard seat. Sounds in the distance—then silence, which was worse. Nothing made sense, and we knew nothing. Somewhere a telephone was ringing. Stopped. Rang again. Stopped.

At one point—on Black Moustache's orders—the shutters were barred, and the sub-machine gun moved out again. The gunner stayed behind, sitting on the desk corner, swinging his left leg to and fro, beating time to an invisible march. He was wearing shapeless baggy trousers, and his rather dirty feet—I remember thinking that my mother wouldn't let *me* go out like that—were buckled into sandals. He looked quite casual, though there was nothing casual about his revolver, or the alert black eyes moving from side to side, watching us, then the doorway, then us again.

Those eyes, between folds of headcloth: eyes in hiding, dangerous, frightened animals. Now and then his gun hand twitched. I sat waiting for it—waiting for the twitch to fire the gun. My throat got drier and drier, with a desert dryness. I was afraid to swallow. What had I been afraid of earlier? Just to spend a whole morning with my father and disappoint him in some way. It seemed odd. Now I longed for him and his rocklike strength. Without expecting to I burst out crying: noisy, tearing sobs, shocking in the twitchy silence. Getting louder.

The girl with purple shoes gripped my hand harder, and whispered, "Hush!" It didn't help, and I couldn't stop. The gunman's eyes moved faster, angrier. The door was slapped wider open and somebody came in. My eyes were full of tears, and the glossy raven-black moustache seemed to swim towards me through them. I shook the tears away, but they kept on coming, with the sobs.

Suddenly, almost forgetting the guns, I dragged my hand free, slipped from the chair, and ran across the room shouting, "Father! I want my Fa! Where is he—where?" My voice sounded shockingly loud, my feet skidded on the highly polished floor. Stiff with terror, I collided with the big man's legs and clung to them tightly, trying to save myself.

"There would be a child! It's bad for the image." He spoke on a high, raw note, full of exasperation, and so like my father that I forgot this was a gunman, opened my mouth, and began bawling like a two-year-old. It was the sort of thing that often started off a scene at home. Now a wiry hand seized my shoulder, and shook me into silence.

"Which of these women is your mother?"

I shook my head. Releasing his legs, which weren't at all comforting, I was free to drag my hands across my blubbered face. He was speaking Arabic, so I answered in the same way: "I'm with my father. He—he's not in here—" I began to cry again, trying to hold it back. For the first time it dawned on me that I might have seen Fa for the last. Here I was, all alone with strange women and these terrorists. I knew they were that—what else could they be? It was all right on TV, not when it was real. We hadn't heard more shots, but some of the guns could be silenced; they often were in books.

"Please, oh please—"

Black Moustache strode to the doorway, shouting, "*Arabi.*"

There were soft running footsteps outside. The man who had carried me upstairs came in. His smile had gone, he looked serious and pale. He just glanced at me, then at his leader. A question mark look.

"Which of that lot has lost a child?"

"He was with the tall fair Englishman, I think."

"The boy's not English—speaks Arabic."

The one called Arabi shrugged. They both looked at me as if they wished I wasn't there. I wished I wasn't, either.

"Mother's Lebanese," I ventured, sniffing. "She's not here. I'm Thomas. Thomas Z. Amsterel. My father's Cornelius K. Amsterel. He—he's very big. And he's in Oil."

Above my head they exchanged looks. For the second time I saw Arabi's flashing grin. "He'd best go to Amsterel—who's so very big. And in Oil."

"No, keep him here with the women."

I moved closer to Arabi. Instinctively I felt he might be more on my side. "Please—*please*. I want to go to Fa. Father, I mean."

Black Moustache shook his head at us. "The men are best together."

"After all, Rashid, he is a man—or will be." That grin again.

"Anyway, he was bawling like a baby." Black Moustache sounded indifferent, though. His mind wasn't on it, I suppose he had a lot to think about. He was staring at the shutters, narrow-eyed. Perhaps he was expecting them to burst apart without warning. He frowned. "Should we have left the Heckler and Koch in here?"

I didn't know what that was, but I supposed it was the sub-machine gun. Funny how I can still remember most of what I was thinking then, in spite of all the confusion. One bit of me noticing things, another crying to be out of there—the bit that had been bawling like a baby; yet another bit aware of my stomach, which was sick, and yet hungry as anything for that promised ice with a kind of desperate dried-up hunger.

"I think the gun's better where it is, covering the hall," said Arabi. Then he added, "Look, he's stopped crying." He smiled at me, though I could still see that pulse beating too fast in his throat.

"Enough of him, anyway." Black Moustache, whose name was Rashid, said it dismissively. Arabi took it as consent. His hand fell to my shoulder, urging me outside the room.

"I must pee," I said desperately, stopping in the passage.

"Can't you hold it?"

"*No.*"

He laughed then. "What do you think I am, your nurse-maid?" He shepherded me along the corridor, till we found a grand tiled lavatory, with a basin and soft towels and soap.

"Hurry up."

The relief was enormous. He stood over me, whistling rather anxiously between his teeth. He barely gave me time to pull my pants up again.

"Rashid will shoot me," he said, as he led me back the way we'd come. On the central landing we passed another gun-man, with the too-familiar sub-machine gun. He was staring over the balusters, down into the black and white marble hall. It was strange how used I was getting to the sight of gunmen. He glanced up in some surprise as Arabi hustled me past him, and on towards another door. It was the men hostages' room. There was still no sign of Uncle Omar—but I saw Fa at once, leaning against the farther wall. I didn't notice anyone else, he alone was real and solid to me. I ran to him, and threw my arms around his legs. I looked up into his face, and it was sort of stretched and shiny, with wetness round his lips like sweat—though the room wasn't hot, it was cool and shady.

"Fa!" I said. "Did you wonder where I was?"

I thought, he's too relieved to speak. He just sighed. One of his arms moved then, stiffly. He placed his hand on my head, like Uncle Omar did with Alley Bear when he was explaining something, or comforting him. Fa's hand weighed heavy, as though his arm wouldn't support it. Heavier than lead. I held on to his legs, to keep from falling down. There was a funny sort of shiver going through them, or perhaps through me,

37

because I was shaking now, not really knowing why, and starting to cry again. Soundlessly, so that black Rashid wouldn't come and get me and put me back among the strange women with their hot, brassy powder smell.

"It's all right, Thomas," is what I thought Fa began to say, in a brash sort of tone, quite loud. I used to think he had the voice a bull would have if it could speak, yet somehow this wasn't his bull voice at all, and it didn't drown out what Arabi was saying to another gunman by the door: "We'll get him out—if we can."

I turned my head to watch him go, half closing the door behind him. Get who out? Me?

There wasn't time to wonder about that, because something else happened immediately—a flurry of noise in the corridor, violence it sounded like, and sharp argument. The door shot wide again, and Uncle Omar was pushed into the room, arms raised above his head. He was all dirty and dishevelled, and blood was seeping from a cut above his forehead—yet when he spoke it was calmly, not put on. You could tell it was real calm from deep inside himself, the sort of calm I'd seen once on his face when I crept into Aunt Sheikhah's room early one day, to see if Alley Bear was there, and instead found Omar sitting crosslegged on a mat before the window. It was funny, but I suddenly remembered how I'd swum with him the whole length of the local swimming baths, when usually I sank halfway and had to be rescued...

"Certainly they will be reasonable," Omar was saying. "Give them time—they are real people, out there. Responsible people. They will consider everything you say, everything you told them when you rang the Press this morning. Just give them time."

I didn't understand, and looked up at Fa, but of course he didn't understand either, not knowing Arabic.

"They'd better be quick about it! Cutting the outside line —is that co-operation?"

"Aren't they rigging a special one? Please wait."

"Wait! Our ends must be achieved, our demands fully met. No compromise." It was a gunman I hadn't seen before who was being so unpleasant. He struck Omar in the small of the back, and he came staggering across the room towards us, landing against the wall with a bruising thud. He was just beside me when he turned, pivoting very slowly, as though testing something out. Everyone else had their hands down already but he asked very, very politely, "May I lower my hands now?" and then lowered them gently, as you might not to rouse the anger of a strange uncertain-tempered dog.

Fa said, "Omar." His knees stopped that strange shivering, or mine did. Ours, perhaps.

"No more talking." Our guard held up his left hand, and we all saw the lemon-shaped object in it, and his finger through the pin.

6 So THE LONG silent hungry waiting began again. I leant against Fa, and kept my eyes on Uncle Omar. He winked at me. I winked back. The corner of his mouth went up in a smile. The guard stared bleakly, till he saw the signals were just for me. All the men were kept standing. I was afraid of being put back with the women, so I kept standing too, as long as I could. At last my legs began to buckle. I slid down, till I knelt with my face pressed against Fa's legs. The stuff of his trousers felt harsh against my cheek. I moved my fingers cautiously, crawling them across a gap till they found and clung to the different-smelling stuff of Uncle Omar's. I pulled it towards me, till my cheek and nose were touching it.

The emptiness in my stomach was a nasty cramping pain. It felt like weeks or months since I'd lost that egg. As though he knew just how I felt, Uncle Omar said: "Surely you'll feed the child? You can't make war on children."

War—was it? I supposed so, if that was what he called it.

"Many of our women and children are hungrier than he is."

Where? I was bewildered. I swivelled round, and saw the guard staring at me. Our eyes met. His voice was just surly, but his eyes—they glared at me across that room reddish and gleaming. It was a look I'd seen once before, in a cheetah at the Zoo.

A moment later Rashid the leader was in our room, saying fiercely, "Did I hear talking? I told you, *no fraternising*."

"That man spoke."

The gun indicated Omar.

"About what? And did you have to answer?"

I was sorry for Fa, who couldn't understand. Not that it was much use knowing.

"The child."

"What with the child?"

"Wants it fed."

"But I thought—it's not his, is it?"

Cheetah-eyes answered, "No," and jerked his head towards Fa on my other side.

Rashid simply shrugged, and went away.

"Fa—" I looked up at him.

"You heard: no talking," said Cheetah-eyes, and held up the hand-grenade. His finger twitched upon the pin.

It was horrid and fascinating: like those big black hairy Zoo spiders made me feel. Altogether there was a lot of Zoo feeling in the room. And loud voices outside in the passage. Tense and rough. Rashid—arguing with Arabi? I couldn't tell. I didn't really care. By this time I was one large dull ache, as well as sick and scared. I wanted Mother and Sheikhah and Bear, and to be out of this horrible place that should have meant ice-cream, but had turned to a nightmare where men with guns and red eyes looked at you hungrily, and nothing made sense, and you weren't allowed to talk or move around or eat.

Footsteps again. Everyone got tense each time that happened. This time it was Arabi who came in. His gun was stuck casually in his waistband, because he was carrying a tumbler and a plate. He put them down in the middle of the floor, as though feeding a dog.

"For Thomas Z," he told Cheetah, not looking at me.

"What's that?"

"For the boy."

"Why? Who said?"

"Rashid. And he can have a chair."

Arabi went away. The Cheetah said—all muffled through his folds of scarf—"Come and get it." His hot red-eyed look was still there, though, so I stayed where I was, my cheek against Omar's trousers. Hunger had left me, and my legs were too pins and needley for me to move easily. If they meant to shoot us all I half-wished they'd get it over. Westerns were always fast-moving. I knew I'd never want to see one again.

It was Omar who dared to speak. "Go on, Thomas. You go and eat while you can."

His smile urged me on, and I unwound myself, saying "Ow", and crawled stiffly like a two-year-old across the floor. I was sure the other prisoners' eyes were on me. I could almost feel them on my back, like hungry insects, twenty-four of them. There were ten other hostages, besides us three. I didn't get them sorted out till later on. They were just men: tall or short, thin or fat, Arab and foreign, with one huge black man who was really straight from Africa, you could tell because he wore flowing coloured robes and a round beaded cap.

They were all silent, obeying that gun and the grenade, but their eyes spoke for them. So I felt really mean as I picked up the things Arabi had brought. Anyway, I would have shared them willingly, I could hardly swallow. It was better when I sipped the watery milk. There must have been an office fridge somewhere, unless the gunmen had actually brought their rations with them. There was something in the milk that tasted odd, it prickled the tip of my tongue and made me feel woozier and as if nothing mattered very much, so I ate the cheesy biscuits, not thinking any longer about Fa and Omar being empty.

Afterwards the Cheetah made the African and another man push a chair against the wall for me, between Fa and Omar. It was a huge, padded, high-backed swivel-chair, and I climbed up into its leather depths, and wound it to its full height, then curled myself up like a puppy. Going round in it had made me feel woozier still. I was just aware that one of the gunmen was coming in and out of the room, taking people to the lavatory as though they were my age, and I was vaguely glad that Fa and Omar weren't taken out together. Then I drowsed into a peculiar half-world of ghost gunmen and high stairs leading to empty, frightening rooms. Dimly ashamed, I wet myself before I slept.

When I woke the room was striped in shadow and harsh brightness. The shutters were closed, and someone had rigged up a standing light, its glare turned full upon us. At first I was scared to find myself alone with Cheetah—but when I raised my head to peer over the chair's rounded leather arm I found that Fa and Omar and the rest were sitting on the floor, backs to the wall.

They looked a strange waxy yellow in the unshaded light, except the African, who was greenish-brown. Fa had a hollow-round-the-eyes and wooden look, as though he was carved out of something hard and lasting. I thought proudly: he's strong, they won't get him down, he'll win. No one had been allowed to smoke, and I hoped he wasn't feeling awful without his usual cigarettes. I was quite glad about the ban otherwise. I didn't like the smell, it made my eyes water.

I turned over towards Uncle Omar, and my careful movement roused him to look up at me, and smile. I felt suddenly glad that we were both in this together, and not him and Alley Bear. He wouldn't have wanted Bear in here anyway—fat, friendly Bear, with his bulging cheeks and blazing acceptance of everyone: Aunt Sheikhah often scolded him for making up to strangers in the streets or park. Then I was sorry for Omar, because he'd been away from them so long just lately, and he must be missing them. And I was sorry for them too, missing him. It was dreadful to think they didn't know he was still safe and sitting here beside me.

There and then I decided to pretend for him that I was Alley Bear, which would be a gain all round. So I pretended hard, and I thought he guessed that I was being Bear. It was like a thread between us, secret comfort that no one else could overhear. Even when he shut his eyes and leaned his head back against the wall I could imagine thoughts going to and fro between us. Then nothing was quite so scaring or so terrible.

Outside the school study window the cat was curled up in shadow, sound asleep. The sparrows had flown. I put my pen down and wrinkled my forehead, trying to dig up something more concrete from the rest of Day One for this perverse task MacArthur had landed me with. I licked the chocolate, letting the bitter flavour linger on my tongue. Was there anything more than fear and growing tension? Bewilderment too—at least for eight-year-old me?

I put the chocolate down, and shoved it aside. Day Four was the real bitter-chocolate day. It was mostly small things I remembered about Day One, after the first shocks. Things like that rigged-up light shining all the time; and the mean feeling I still had after more semi-starvation supper of weak milk and biscuits, while everyone else had nothing but nasty-looking tea. This time no one had laced my milk with anything but water.

Yet I was sleepy anyway. I do remember staring at Uncle Omar's face just before I slept. His eyes were closed, he looked peaceful, not like a prisoner at all. He'd wiped his face clean of blood, just a thin edge of cut showed beneath his hairline. He was smiling—or that might have been a trick of light drawing lines of shadow at the corners of his mouth. I also remember thinking that things couldn't really be so bad if Uncle Omar looked like that. I was still watching him when I went to sleep.

7 I WOKE ON Day Two with a scream so loud that it echoed through my head after I stopped screaming.

My mouth was still wide open when two terrorists burst into the room, shouting at us and each other, guns swivelling wildly.

"Was it just that child?"

"Bloody brat—" Arabic, of course.

I sat bolt upright, shivering, scared they'd shoot.

Fa's hand was on my arm, gripping it warningly.

"All right now? All right, Thomas?" he was saying.

Uncle Omar's deep voice spoke up on my other side: "He was dreaming. Only a dream."

The gunmen subsided then, muttering among themselves, giving us dark glances. But Omar's tone had soothed them down. I looked at him thankfully. His wide comforting smile. It was such a relief to see him like that—not as I'd just seen him in that terrible dream: blood at the corners of his mouth, and eyes rolled upward, staring.

I gulped out: "Uncle Omar, I want to go home, I want home!" The gunmen were still there, three of them counting Cheetah who was still on guard, but I couldn't stop—kept chanting louder and louder, "I want to go home, I want Mother and Aunt Sheikhah and Bear, I want to go home."

"Shut him up, can't you?" Cheetah's voice of menace.

Bit of a memory blank here—till I was sitting on Omar's knees, as Bear might have done, his arm round me, his moustache and bristly chin brushing my cheek. "We'll be going home soon," he said in my ear. "Just as soon as these gentlemen have done a little talking with our friends outside."

45

He murmured, quieter still: "The police are out there now." I don't know if he knew or guessed.

I clutched his hand. "And you?"

"All of us, I expect."

I didn't like that "expect". "Not without you," I whispered. I was still seeing that dream-face, all bloodied. I looked round, shrinkingly, and caught my Fa's expression.

"And Fa." But it was late. I'd failed again in a number one duty—son's duty to his father. He looked away from me, and I felt awful. How could I bear to explain about the dream, and Uncle Omar's face? My Fa's was waxy-yellow in the pale glare of that rigged-up lamp. His sprouting fair beard wasn't so noticeable as Omar's blue-black one, but in a way he looked worse, dried skin peeling at the edges of his lips. He was usually smoking by this time, my mother kept boxes of cigarettes everywhere, in case he ran out.

The gunmen weren't going to be mother to anybody, I could see that, and Rashid, their leader, least of all. He came into the room then with a sort of jaunty, military step. He looked less edgy, though just as frightening. He stood in the middle of the room, issuing commands: one of the guards to stay, Cheetah and the other to shove off and get an hour's sleep. He sounded like a sergeant major. Once they'd gone, he looked us up and down (just like my English teacher did before saying, "Pencils and paper ready for dictation. Who can spell 'Battleship'?").

He had eyes rather like hers too, bleak as dagger points. "It seems that our three just demands are under consideration," he told us with an air of satisfaction. "In the meantime, no harm will come to anyone. Continue to obey your guards, and make no trouble for yourselves. What you were told yesterday remains in force."

Yesterday? Three just demands? All that must have been while I was with the women—no one had told them anything at all. I remembered what my mother sometimes said about the Arab view of women. Rashid had spoken Arabic, and afterwards he made a rough translation into English, which he pronounced very oddly. I could see Fa strain to understand. No one liked to ask questions, they just looked at Rashid's right hand curled round one of those lemon-shaped grenades. It was ready armed, live, and we were within feet of it. Not a specially nice feeling when you'd had no breakfast to buoy you up.

I was still sitting on Omar's knee when Rashid marched out, and I just breathed into his ear: "Who are they really—what do they want? And why *us*?"

"They say they're the Free Army of United Arabia," he breathed back. "As for us—well, we just happened to be in the right place at the right time for them, I'm afraid. As to what they want—quite a lot of things."

"Is that what 'just demands' is?"

"Well—'demands', anyway. You see, some of their friends are in prison, and they want them out. Then they themselves want an aircraft to fly them out of Britain, and a bus to the airport."

"You and Fa could buy them tickets, couldn't you?"

"It's not quite so simple, I'm afraid."

"You mean they want more?" It seemed to me the gunmen were being rather greedy. "They could have our tickets for Beirut," I whispered. "That's three to start with."

"There are seven of them. And yes, they want more. They want a statement of their views on the BBC. And they want the questions of Palestine and the Kurds raised at the United Nations, with a promise of backing from Britain and the whole of Europe."

I didn't understand really what he meant, but it sounded like an awful lot, rather like my list for Christmas, and I never got all of that, only something here and there. It seemed to me we'd be here for ever.

"I want to go to the lavatory," I said. I'd felt loose inside anyway, since seeing that grenade, and now it was worse.

Our guard was looking at us. He was younger than Cheetah, and had ordinary eyes. He wasn't all muffled up, either.

I said it again, very loud. The guard grinned. He gave me quite a friendly look and went to the door and shouted. It was Arabi who came to shepherd me out and down the corridor.

"Always your nursemaid, aren't I?" He leaned against the door, smoking, while I took down my pants. He smoked rather cautiously, as though he didn't want anyone to know. I hoped he wouldn't let Fa see him, it might send him mad.

At first I couldn't get started, not at all.

"Hurry up, can't you?"

Tears filled my eyes. "I can't. I want to, but it won't."

He laughed then. "All right, don't hurry. I'm not going to shoot you in here, you know."

"I don't want to be shot *anywhere*," I said—rather daringly, but he sounded friendly. "It's horrible to talk of shooting people just like that." My insides were working now, but I hardly noticed. "You wouldn't want to be shot, would you? And you wouldn't want people shouting at you, and shutting you in a room and making you hungry and—"

"Now that's enough, you," he said. "Plenty of my people are shut up in worse than these rooms, and go hungry. That's what it's all about."

"Where?" I asked. "Where are they shut up?" I wondered if they were on the upper floor somewhere. Perhaps they were miserable and hungry and dirty in an attic?

"May Allah give patience! I'm not handing you a political lecture here and now! Get a move on."

I pulled up my pants hastily, and he threw his cigarette down the pan, then prodded me back along the corridor and thrust me into our room. "Rashid can take him on next time," he told our guard. "He's a born politician." The guard laughed, and Arabi went away.

"All right, Thomas?" Fa asked, as I returned to my chair.

"Yes, Fa."

That deep chair felt like my only refuge. I peered over its side at Omar, who was leaning back with his eyes shut, looking miles away—I wondered where. And what he was thinking of, though I could guess, really. It was sad that the imaginary thread between us was broken because I truly wasn't Bear, and I felt small and alone. And on the outside looking in again. Only it was worse feeling like that in here, under the glaring light and a terrorist's eye. Not to mention his gun.

Nothing much happened for a while. It may only have been half an hour, but it felt like forever. At last someone brought us some tea, lukewarm without milk, but with quite a lot of sugar. I ate biscuits again, while all the prisoners watched me hungrily. It made me feel so guilty that I was beginning to hate biscuits.

But later a scrawny-looking gunman, one I thought of as Starved Cat, put his head round the door, saying tonelessly, in Arabic then English, "Food will be sent in for everyone by one o'clock. It's definite. Our leader says so. Whatever else happens." He seemed quite glad himself, perhaps they hadn't eaten either. Our guard looked more cheerful too, not so jumpy, although the fingers of his gunhand still gripped so hard that the knuckles stood out white and splintery-looking, just like cooked chicken bones. It seemed amazing that that little dark rod in his hand gave him such power that none of us dared move.

I perked up a bit after that good news about the food, until I saw that there were pearls of sweat on Fa's forehead, and that made my perkish feeling disappear quicker than it came. Just as though he'd spoken I knew that something horrid had been told them, when I was outside with Arabi. It must tie up with "whatever else happens". So we were waiting for something else now, and everyone knew about it except me . . .

I remember I was puzzling over this when I grew aware of a distant sound that was getting at my mind like the irritating buzzzz of a wasp or bee stuck on a window-pane. It was a road drill not far away—punctuated now and then by an extra 'ker-boom, ker-boom' from one of those heavy pneumatic drills that hop up and down like giant frogs so that even the brawniest workman hops with it. People were out there, mending a road. Such an ordinary thing going on in the bright day outside that we couldn't see. Our guard had heard it too. He kept biting his lip and glancing nervously towards the shutters. It puzzled me, and I did hope he wouldn't forget what he was doing with his gun—his hand looked none too steady.

Soon the noise stopped, and he relaxed, and I did too. That is, till I overheard Fa mutter something above my head to Uncle Omar, and I caught the last word: "deadline".

Deadline? *Dead*.

That was it, then. If no one agreed to what the gunmen wanted. It would be some time after one, because anyway we were getting food by then. And then that deadline with threats attached to it—fuses to a time bomb!—was definitely set.

I couldn't reach Fa's hand. I began to cry silently, looking through my tears at Uncle Omar—but he was sitting with his eyes shut, far away in thought. I began to bawl.

"Hush, be quiet, Thomas!"

I could hardly hear Fa trying to calm me through my bawl, it was getting louder. I wanted to stop it now but couldn't, it would be dreadful if they killed us because my mouth wouldn't shut—

Rashid erupted into the room. That's how it seemed, anyway. My bawl stopped. My mouth stayed open, stuck.

He flicked a furious glance at me. It almost stung.

"He's only a child," said Omar, softly apologetic. "And very overtired."

50

"We'll get rid of him," snapped Rashid. A pulse beat in his forehead, bulging up and down. I had a frog once which bulged like that when it breathed, but my frog wasn't angry, it was frightened. "If they'd been more responsible, less hostile, he would have gone before."

"They" must be the world outside—ordinary friendly world, so oddly lost and distant. How dreadful of it to be hostile, when that meant I couldn't go home to mother, Sheikhah and Bear. I might have guessed, me being under-sized and with some experiences already of my own.

My mouth came unstuck. I swallowed, and just managed, "Fa!"

"It's almost time," Rashid was saying.

Fa's head was cocked. He was listening, but not to me. I listened too, and heard a distant babble, then running foot-steps. Starved Cat with a terrorist I hadn't seen before—scrawny too—burst into the room. They looked white round the eyes and prickly with dark beard. Cutlasses would have turned them into pirates—Rashid was the pirate king, he scared them too.

"They're coming!"

"They're early," said Rashid, calm and cold. "So let them wait. I want no—accidents."

"Come here," he said.

It was a moment before I realised he meant me. My stomach nose-dived, and I shrank farther into my armchair.

"Now, Thomas, do as you're told. At once," said Fa warningly.

His face had gone an ashy colour, not too good with his fair wavy hair. Sometimes my mother's friends went on and on about Fa's marvellous looks, and I wondered what they'd think now, when he was so grey with fear for me.

I unwound myself slowly, and went to stand before Rashid, not daring to look up at him; keeping my eyes on his pale khaki trousers. I can still see the exact pattern of their zig-zag weave, and the strand of fluff where a snagged thread was hanging loose. The grenade in his strong brown hand was only a few centimetres from my nose.

("We'll get rid of him". Was this *it*?)

"Right. Take him down now."

"Come on, kid."

I was so rigid with terror that First Cat had to steer me, pushing me ahead of him. I glanced back just in time to catch Fa's jerky smile, Omar's dark eyes watching me, his smile, his hand raised in a goodbye wave.

The sub-machine gun was still set up on the circular landing above the staircase well. Someone had daubed huge slogans in purple chalk around the cream-and-gold-papered walls. Scrawls of Arabic, loops and swirls and dots fiercely stabbed right through into the plaster. The hall was shiny with reflecting marble under the lit though broken chandelier. Some of its lights lay shattered on the floor. They must have been knocked off when the plaster fell.

Two armed figures, very still, their heads and mouths muffled in red and white kuffiehs, stood either side of the great hall door, a little back from it, their cocked guns covering the space between.

In the hall centre, directly beneath the chandelier, lay a sort of improvised stretcher. A huddled form was lying on it—the Security Guard who had been shot. He looked ...dead. I drew back, and First Cat gripped my arm and dragged me down the stairs. I wanted to look away but couldn't, I could only stare and stare. I hardly noticed the woman standing by the stretcher.

We reached the bottom of the flight, and then I saw the guard was breathing in shallow gasps, and his eyelids fluttered. One arm was bandaged to his chest with strips of torn white towel, splashed with red. There was a patch of brownish-red just below it too.

First Cat led me across the hall. The woman was swaying

as though she wanted to fall down, like a top at the end of turning. Her right hand was pressed against her back, and her huge round stomach made her look top-shaped too. I'd noticed her among the other women, she was clumsier and fatter than my mother.

"Here—take his hand."

She didn't, she just stared at me. Her eyes showed whiteness all round prune centres. Two plump little hands hung down, pink fruits, gleaming greasily with sweat. They'd be all slithery and soft to hold. I didn't want to be got rid of, dead or alive, in their clutches, and I could see she felt the same about me. She began making an odd noise beneath her breath: "Mi-mi-mi," on and on: "mi-mi-mi", so soft you could hardly hear it, except when her teeth clicked, little white rabbit-teeth, chattering against each other.

Second Cat, who'd followed me downstairs, glanced at his watch, then at the door. Nothing happened for a moment, till a distant clock began chiming twelve.

Together both Cats crouched suddenly to hoist the stretcher upward. I don't think it was heavy, it was made of broken chair-backs, lashed together, but the guard was bulky, and the way they jerked it made him groan. At the same time I heard footsteps above, looked up, and saw Arabi walk on to the landing. The hall dimmed as he switched off the lights. I could just see him as a darker blotch beside the sub-machine gun's muzzle poking through the balusters.

One terrorist was unbarring the hall door, it was swinging open. "Hurry!" He jerked his head at the woman, who began to totter forward. I saw her outlined against the daylight, plump as a plum, and beyond her two men in dark blue were crouched outside the threshold, looking in.

The woman was between them now, swaying from side to side, a slowing top. They jumped to catch her as she toppled sideways. First and Second Cats moved forward, then lowered the stretcher and gave it a tremendous shove. The wounded guard cried out as it shot through the doorway, skidding over the marble as if it were a sledge.

"You too," said First Cat, pushing me forward.

I went a few steps, then wavered in the sudden glare of daylight, pinned there by an amazing thousand eyes. So many people's eyes—police eyes, lens eyes...guns' eyes. Guns each side of me. Speared in a thicket of eyes I stood in plain view, shielding my own with my arm. I knew a mighty thunder of guns would all fire together as I was going, I should be full of holes as a colander.

A voice cried, "Come on, kid, quick—outside."

"What's he waiting for?"

My feet seemed stuck to the floor. Fa always told me to jump off the diving board and I never could.

Just then a distant car backfired, like a gun going off. I turned and dodged between the Cats' legs, darting through the hallway for the stairs.

8 BEHIND ME THE Cats were swearing in full flood. I didn't even look at them, just ran on and up and up until I reached the landing.

Arabi was still there, looking down. He put a hand out to stop me. I was breathing hard, in great pants. He didn't speak, yet somehow I knew that he knew why I ran. We stood there side by side, his hand on my shoulder, both of us staring towards the hall door, where the exchange was over: woman and wounded guard out, two long crates of food in. The door was slammed shut again and barred, while the two Cats turned towards the stairs.

I edged out from beneath Arabi's hand, and scuttled away along the landing—away from his too-seeing eyes. Furious with myself for not escaping to my safe ordinary world again. Sick with misery and shame because I knew just why I hadn't.

In the hostage room a gun muzzle swung to cover me. Then the terrorist's brows shot up in mild surprise, and he waved me back towards my old familiar place. I crept across the open floor, not looking at Fa or Omar, and met the African's gaze instead. His face creased into a wide grin, and he clapped his hands at me approvingly. It was friendly, but I felt too bleak to care. I climbed hastily into the leather chair and turned my face away so that Omar couldn't see straight through me as Arabi had. I met Fa's gaze instead.

First Cat followed me back into the room.

"Your accursed child wouldn't go—" He switched into English, seeing Fa's blank expression. "Your boy ran back to you, we could not wait longer." He looked both angry and upset.

"Well done, Thomas." Fa's large firm hands patted me on the arm. I hadn't seen that expression on his face before. My running into danger not to leave them was real credit. That made me feel worse, angry with him and with myself. I wished we were both dead, so fiercely that I was scared in case my thoughts were strong enough to explode a hand grenade.

Omar's voice said urgently: "You'll try again later, surely?"

"That's for Rashid—for our leader. It's no fault of ours there was a child here."

Fa muttered something beneath his breath.

"But you cannot—I mean, with so little time—" There was greater urgency in Omar's voice. I'd never heard him lost for words before. I looked from Fa to him and back again— Fa's forehead was still sweating. That deadline. How could I have forgotten for one moment? We were all for the high jump soon. I'd run straight back into the danger, whatever it was and whenever it would be.

"It is for Rashid," repeated First Cat obstinately.

Omar just nodded. I knew already that he wasn't one for arguing. He made up his mind, spoke quietly, then let it go at that. I felt sure he'd never, ever yelled to get his way, on and on, like I did sometimes, half wanting Fa to cuff me and end my bawl, which sometimes kept going till I couldn't stop.

I saw now that all our fellow hostages were looking very down in the mouth. I'd hardly noticed them before, they were just a lot of sweaty strangers, prickly with beard, all in the same mess with us. I'd noticed the African because he'd smiled at me quite often, and looked as though it wasn't all put on for show. Sitting between him and Fa were a Fat Man and a Lean Man: one all jelly wobbles and Ave Marias— Italian, maybe? The other wearing worry beads around his wrist, and with squinty little eyes which flickered to and fro from gun to door and back again. They were like meat flies.

Suddenly the door was pushed open violently. We all jumped, thinking this was it, but it was only Second Cat helping Rashid with one of the opened food crates. They pushed it into the middle of the room.

Rashid said: "You can eat. And I tell you, maybe you have more time now. A note came with the food. We have not considered yet, but maybe they come to terms. It is more promising, that's all I say."

Then he told our guard to go and get some sleep. (They took their catnaps in turn, and probably ate that way too. I thought of Cheetah, curled up like an animal in a bush.) First Cat was left to cover us, and Rashid went away, telling Second Cat to start doling out the food. I heard their names for the first time. They were Yahia and Yusuf.

Everyone was looking much more cheerful now, since Rashid's speech, and Yusuf and Yahia were quite friendly. Yusuf began calling us out one by one. He spoke Arabic mostly and, when people didn't understand, used gestures. His English was hardly there. It took quite a time, because there were thirteen of us altogether. You could tell by the way people moved that they never forgot the guns or the grenade.

The first two to be called were Directors of Uncle Omar's grandfather's firm. I knew who they were because they'd met him at the airport and brought him to our flat when he arrived in England.

They looked very boring and very smooth, most unlike my handsome, tall and rangy father. They were the sort of people I didn't want to be, if I ever did grow up. Now that they had to obey someone like scruffy Yusuf they didn't look half so pleased with themselves. They grabbed their food, and whipped back to their places fast as light.

The next two were younger copies of them—both terribly neat, with sleek wavy hair. You could hardly tell them apart, except that one wore a beard and the other a moustache. I felt they spent a lot of time grooming themselves, and it was too

57

bad that they were all blue-skinned and prickly now. After them came a sad-looking bald man, who looked as though he'd had a saddish bald kind of life, and a bold-looking youth who was anything but bald, with a lot of fuzz everywhere—cheeks and chin, hands and skinny wrists, and even escaping in wiry curls above his tie. I felt he might bounce, in better circumstances.

I asked Uncle Omar who they were, and he whispered back something about clerks and computers which I didn't really get. I never got their names sorted out either. Most of the hostages were Company employees, or Company wives. One or two were clients, and caught in the net like Fa and me . . .

"Mr. Bedrawi," Yusuf was saying.

Beside me Uncle Omar drew in his breath sharply. Fa heard him—I saw him glance at Omar and then stare hard at this man Bedrawi. I stared too, and thought I'd seen him somewhere before—but it was only the vaguest feeling, I couldn't place him. The bald man was staring too, and the bouncy one, chewing his full red underlip as though he had to get a grip on something. Uncle Omar's senior staff were looking at their shoes.

Mr. Bedrawi was getting to his feet, calm and slow—yet there was something about his calm that was put on, unlike Omar's. He had a long oval face, very firm lips, a curved nose. Good-natured maybe, though giving nothing away. Sometimes you can tell a lot about people just by looking at them, and sometimes it's easier with strangers than with your own family. When I was eight I spent a good deal of time wondering if they ever felt so small and lost as me, and who they were inside, and how they got that way. I guessed a lot—for instance, I guessed that Mr. Bedrawi's big thick spectacles weren't there just because he needed them, but also to stop the world looking too closely into his eyes and seeing things it shouldn't see.

He was bland, that was it: bland as banana custard. Yet I felt there was something secret beneath the blandness—and maybe it was that secret which made Omar draw in his breath, and gave Fa that considering look.

He was certainly taking his time about everything. I'm sure it was his habit, and he felt people must wait for him. Yusuf got all fidgety, and Yahia's fingers were pretty fidgety on his gun. Still, they both waited in silence while Mr. Bedrawi hovered over the food, looking for the best. His nose-tip was mole-ish, quivering for special titbits. He pounced at last, drew out a paper napkin too, and flourished it disdainfully in Yusuf's face, before turning his back on them and settling down in his own place with such an air of satisfaction that he might have been sitting down to eat in his own home.

I held my breath—almost waiting for them to shoot him. But Yusuf angrily called out the African. He was followed by the Fat Man—Señor Juan something, so he was Spanish, not Italian—and then the Lean Man with the flicking eyes and worry beads. He was so scared he was quick as an oiled eel. And then it was Fa's turn, and mine.

Yusuf called us out together, and in spite of that awful Deadline feeling in my mind and stomach I was glad to find the crate was still half full. There was Arab and English food. Whoever was outside watching the house had been quite clever, had done their homework, Fa would have said. I suppose they'd whistled up a Lebanese restaurant, and it was meant to keep Rashid and his gang good-tempered.

"Do you really want that awful stuff, Thomas?" muttered Fa, when I chose *falafel* and *kosharee* and stuffed vineleaves instead of the ham and hard-boiled eggs that he was taking.

"Feed him and get on, English," snapped Yahia, "we don't run a café here," but he shot me an approving look.

We scuttled back to our places. Omar went last, and then Yusuf doled out mugs of wine and water, mixed. The Directors looked cross, I thought—perhaps the wine was theirs.

Both the gunmen were drinking too, and my mug of water was cough-cure pink. Uncle Omar took pure water, he was very strict with himself about that, being Muslim; and so the rest of his firm, when they saw him do that, stuck to water too, in a regretful and rather shamefaced way. Even the Directors. Mr. Bedrawi, the Spaniard, the African, and the Lean Man swigged wine as eagerly as Fa. People began to talk together, and the terrorists pretended not to hear.

When I'd finished eating, I noticed the bouncy clerk had dropped his butter and was sitting on it. I wanted to share this excellent joke with Omar, but he didn't look up when I nudged him. He hadn't eaten much, he just sat staring into his glass as though seeing pictures in it. The way he stared made me uneasy. There was a kind of patient sadness in it, as if he was accepting something that he didn't like.

"Uncle Omar—"

"Thomas?" He spoke so strangely, I didn't feel he was there inside himself at all.

The joke about the butter didn't seem so funny. I said: "Aren't you going to eat? It's good."

"Is it?" He put the glass down. He still had that funny clouded look when he glanced at Mr. Bedrawi and the gunmen.

"They may come and take it away if you don't hurry," I whispered.

He smiled then, in his old way. "Thanks, Thomas—I mustn't waste it while it's there, must I?"

In the end, there was no hurry. Arabi came loping into the room, to say something in an undertone to Yahia, who looked as pleased as his starved-cat face would let him.

"Wish I spoke the damn tongue," murmured Fa fretfully. "What's going on, Thomas?" He disliked asking me, I could see that.

"I couldn't hear, Fa," I whispered thankfully. Just then Arabi turned towards us, and began to speak slowly and formally, translating each phrase into English as he went along.

"Your Home Secretary himself has intervened to ask for an extension of the Deadline, so that all our points may be more fully considered. Since it is possible we have a positive situation by tonight, Rashid has agreed. In the meantime, we will try to make you as comfortable as possible. We intend harm to nobody, please understand that. Does anybody wish to ask a question?" His smile just lifted the corners of his moustache. "I don't promise to answer, of course."

Several people spoke at once. He laughed with real amusement.

He must feel they're going to get whatever they're on about, I thought. Soon we shall be out of this, not dirty smelly frightened hostages any more.

"You first." Arabi pointed at the Spaniard, who was so agitated that he made several false starts before he came out with: "My wife! I must see my wife——"

Arabi looked uncomfortable and shook his head. "Rashid has decided that men and women stay apart. He thinks it right. For everyone."

"Right!" The Spaniard was almost bouncing up and down on his behind. "You have no right——"

Arabi just looked down at his gun, and Señor Juan sank back with an empty sort of gesture, sad and defeated.

"You should at least let my son go now," said Fa. "Wouldn't your—your leader let me take him out, if I promised to return? You saw, he wouldn't go without me."

Arabi hesitated. He looked at me, and said, "Since we make that attempt, a vote has been taken."

"On what—on keeping a *child* here—and some women?" Uncle Omar sounded astounded.

"Four of us take the view that they are a strong bargaining counter, and Rashid himself has hardened on it." Arabi looked less cool, I thought, and not so happy. He was a bit pink under his skin. I was sure he wasn't one of the four—and perhaps he regretted asking if anyone had questions.

"Is there a further Deadline set?"

"Won't you release anyone at all?"

Both of the Directors spoke at once, and he replied, "Yes— at ten tomorrow morning. As to who—if anyone—is released, Rashid will decide that later."

Mr. Bedrawi hadn't spoken yet. Now he said—sounding scared, I thought—"But you will let us *all* go—once your demands are met?" Like Arabi, he seemed to think the terrorists had won.

"Perhaps—some of you. We've asked for a bus to take us to the airport, and then a plane to Libya. Even when that's granted, we still have to protect ourselves, our wives and families. If we do not have to—" He looked at me again, and stopped, and then went on quickly, "If we win, you will still, all of you, be a strong shield against reprisals."

Mr. Bedrawi looked taken aback. There was a general groan of dismay, and Arabi added gently, "In the end, you'll be freed. We'll keep our word on that—if your Government keeps theirs."

My *kosharee* started to revolve, it seemed stuck, like my egg on that first day. I didn't like flying, anyway. My mother hated it too. She always made me sit by her, and I could feel shivers going down her arm, which then went up my arm, as well. Bear loved planes, I knew. Aunt Sheikhah had said so. I could just see Bear bouncing fatly on her lap when he was smaller, while she sat holding him, smelling of her strong sweet scent. Perhaps it wouldn't be so bad if I could hold Uncle Omar's hand at take-off.

"You don't seem troubled about our wives and families," said Fa angrily.

"We'll do our best for you, and them," replied Arabi, but he sounded uncomfortable, I thought. And he left the room quickly.

The rest of the day dragged. The siege seemed to have been going on for ever, and what was strangest of all was that it was so dull when it wasn't extremely nasty. I can remember thinking a lot about Bear, wondering if he was grizzling on and on because we hadn't come home; and I wondered if my mother and Aunt Sheikhah were out there in the street somewhere, waiting for real news of us, waiting and waiting for our rescue or release. It seemed impossible that quite near at hand everything must be going on as usual—people shopping and walking dogs, and quarrelling for no good reason. I do remember thinking that I'd never row again if I got outside. Not with anyone. I haven't kept to that, of course.

Another thing I vividly recall is crouching by the African, half enveloped in his flowing robe, gazing up into his face while he told me a story, very quietly, so that Yahia shouldn't get all jumpy and wave his gun about.

It was a longish story, a green story, that's how I think of it now, because that's how it was then: plantations came into it, and sugar-cane, and jungle, sappy and drippy with creeper. It was a true story too, about his ancestors, how they were stolen away to America, and the story changed colour in the middle, harsh and cold and grey-blue while they crossed the sea.

" . . . chained to each other, lying in rows, face to face so they felt each other's breath, heard each other's moans. People died in each other's arms—" He spoke in a long slow dreamy drawl, as though it was happening right there in front of him.

"—yes, they made love like that, Thomas, love on one side, death on the other—" His long thin hands gripped my forearms, while I stared up at him, seeing behind his dark intense face a flutter of parrots' wings, crocodiles, seas like walls of blue glass, black people tossing and turning in the wave's overhang, twisting and writhing under the white man's lash and the blaze of a burning sun which turned to silver the snow-white puffs of cotton on the rows of cotton plants—

It was all the shuddery things in one that I sensed and dreaded about life, and it spun from his lips in a long thin thread of sound with a sweetness of tone that might have made fairground spun sugar of it, if it hadn't been so dreadful.

"It didn't really happen," I said, sudden and quick and fierce.

"What? What's that?" The eyes that had smiled at me so merry and well-wishing were long black slits like knives.

"It didn't, it didn't! His name wasn't Clem and he wasn't whipped, he stayed in that jungle with the parrots and the —and the—and his name was Nkomo, it wasn't Clem. It never happened, they didn't take them, they didn't put them in a plane—" I wrenched myself from his grasp, and threw myself across the room till I lay weeping in Uncle Omar's arms. Beyond myself totally, as my mother would have said; not caring if it was a slavemaster's whip or a gun in Yahia's hand.

I was sobbing and crying and carrying on like anything, and even Fa hissing at me across the empty chair, "Thomas —do behave yourself, Thomas," couldn't make me stop.

Funny—but that storm of emotion is the very last thing I can dig from my memory about Day Two. It's as if my tears swept everything else away, except the sense of Uncle Omar holding me as though I was Bear, while threads of sympathy crept towards me from some hostages, along with black annoyance and disapproval from the rest.

9 THE ROOM ALWAYS felt specially airless by night, and it smelt of unwashed people. Most of us tossed and turned and some of us snored. The younger of the two clerks cried sometimes; to hear a grown man cry like that made a pit open in my stomach—or that's how it felt.

I slept curled up in my chair with Fa's jacket over me. He himself lay on a Persian rug, isolated, except that the tearful clerk's head rested on one end so that he lay sprawled like a crusader dog at Fa's feet. By the rigged light I could watch them both: the clerk's face round, bristly and tearstained, barred by his flourishing black moustache, and Fa looking carved and noble, waves of hair flowing strongly back from his high square forehead. His lips were always firmly closed. His face seemed right under his control even when he was asleep. Surely nothing bad could happen to us while he looked like that?

By night, two guards watched us. The door was left wide open, and light from the corridor was regularly broken by the passing to and fro of another terrorist on guard: a black shape with a rifle slung across his shoulder. It was strange how quickly I grew used to sleeping and waking and sleeping again to the sound of a terrorist's padding footfalls and the sobbing of the clerk. On the night following Day Two I slept quite well. I was too worn out to do anything else, in spite of what might happen and where we were.

On Day Three I woke confused. Something had jolted me awake, and it wasn't just a sense of Deadline, the ominous threat of ten o'clock.

Someone's hand was gently shaking me. I sat up, expecting

Fa or Omar, but they were nowhere to be seen and it was Arabi's face close to mine, his gun's hard shininess within centimetres of my nose. He was grinning broadly. I could see how sharp and even his teeth were, very white against his taut brown skin. He had one of these very large Arab noses that stick out at you like signposts (for snuffing their damn way across the desert, Fa always said) and it was almost touching mine. We could have rubbed noses, if we'd wanted to.

"Ai-yah! Good sleeper you are, Thomas Zed!"

"Is it ten—*is* it?" I looked round wildly. "Where—where? Fa! Omar!" I began to struggle off the chair.

Arabi stuck out an arm to push me back. He barely had to touch me, the arm was all solid muscle. He was like a coiled spring, far more powerful than he looked. I shot back in the chair, a snooker ball touched by a master's cue His hand rested on my shoulder, pinning me there.

"Sha, sha. Why should a chip like you worry about ten o'clock, eh? That's better, no need to fuss. The gentlemen are only out there, talking, answering a few questions. I have some orange juice for you."

He had crouched down beside me, balancing himself lightly on his heels. He was still smiling. I couldn't see those pulses beat in his neck, that had shown so when he carried me upstairs. Perhaps there was no Deadline, after all. And Arabi was saying so, saying, "There's no ten o'clock to fear now —all goes better."

"Better? You mean Fa and Omar—we can all go, soon?"

"Come," he said lightly, ignoring that. "Come sit by me, till they return."

Several of the other hostages were missing too. I couldn't see the older members of my uncle's firm, nor Mr. Bedrawi.

Arabi stood up in one swift movement, light and controlled. All his movements were like that, as though they flowed out from the very centre of himself, effortless. A red setter moves like that, or a horse.

I wasn't sure if I should sit with the enemy, but the chair felt big and alone there by the wall, and the remaining hostages had drawn apart, grouped towards the big desk near the window. No one was paying me attention.

The shutters had been pushed ajar so that cool air was coming in. Things were certainly better, and Arabi had come to talk to me, so he hadn't scorned me for my cowardice. Perhaps it was all right to go and sit with him? More practically, he'd no grenade. So I followed obediently across the room and squatted down beside him on an edge of rolled-up rug, though I kept eyeing him sideways: his shiny rod of gun, the taut brown hand loosely holding it.

"Well, Thomas Zed? What are you staring at so hard?"

I didn't want to say "your gun", so I said, "your hand."

He had hands with square fingernails, fine-boned. His gun-hand had a dark ochre-ish mark running slantwise from wrist to forefinger, and when he tapped lightly on the gun barrel the mark wriggled like a wireworm among fine dark hairs. He was watching me solemnly, but I could sense amusement.

I pointed at the mark. "What's that? How did you get it—it's a scar, isn't it?"

"Ah." His nostrils went pinched, and then blew out again. A horse does that when it snuffs your hand. I thought, he *is* a desert horse. "Not in a do like this one."

"What sort of a do, then?"

He considered. Then he told me a story so tall that neither of us could have believed it for a second, though both of us enjoyed it, at least I thought so. It was all flight and fight and dagger-thrust, a dazzling blue dusk, and a lovely girl with huge dark eyes. "Like a gazelle's," he said, and his own eyes crinkled at the corners, so that I knew he didn't expect me to believe him; he was laughing at us both.

"It's not true, is it? You're making it up."

He laughed outright, and the other hostages turned to

stare. "No, no, it's not true—though there was a woman with dark eyes, she was my mother, and she was very cross with me. I put my hand through a window and cut it so badly, I had to go to hospital—I was just a bit older than you must be, now."

"I'm eight. It wasn't nice to be cross."

"She was scared. People are often cross when they're scared. The more scared they are, the crosser they get."

I thought that over. It felt true; perhaps even tough ugly Rashid was so unpleasant because he was scared? Sometimes I screamed and bawled when I was scared, and kicked the floor as if I was Bear's age, till I ended up in bed with no supper. In disgrace, Fa said.

"Were you ever scared? Really scared, I mean?"

"Of course." He slanted a look at me, and added gravely, "You were really scared yesterday, weren't you? Too scared to go, when you had the chance?"

I looked at my dirty knees, and nodded sadly.

"It was the guns, wasn't it?"

Again I nodded. "They were all pointing . . ." I whispered. I saw again the two terrorists, heads muffled, either side of the door, and the figures crouched outside covering me.

"A lot of men run, their first time in battle."

Men. I felt a bit better.

"This isn't a battle, though."

"Isn't it? In a way it is. And one in which *you* didn't have a gun." He shifted his nearer me on his knee, and moved it round a little so that I could see its whole length. It had a kind of quality that matched the hand—wireworm scar and all.

"Do you want to touch it, Thomas Zed?"

I didn't want anything to do with it, but I wouldn't show I was afraid. I put out my hand hesitantly—it looked dwarfed beside his large one—and closed my fingers on the barrel.

"It won't go off, will it?"

He laughed a second time, reassuringly. "Not without some help from me."

I stroked the steel timidly. It grew warm from my touch, felt fierce and silky as an animal, almost alive. It was only kept from preying on things by that hand with the scar.

"My little boy is scared of guns too, Thomas Zed." He sighed. His free hand rose to his shirt pocket, then fell.

"I'm only called Thomas, ever."

"Never—what is it? Tommy? Not even by your father?"

I shook my head. "Always Thomas. He doesn't like names made short."

"I see. Yes—your father. The big man in Oil." He smiled a lopsided smile.

"I'm thirsty," I said. "Where's the orange juice?"

It was a mug of real orange by his side, and he passed it over to me. I drained it, the tip of my nose so far inside the mug that it got sticky. I wiped it on the back of my hand.

"Does your little boy like orange? Is his name Arabi too?"

"Yes, he loves orange. And no, his name's Feisal—Arabi is not my real name, anyway, it's a battle name, one I take in memory of an Egyptian hero, and also of a great wise man who was Arabian too."

I didn't want to think of battles, or brave men. "Is he as old as me?"

"He's younger, quite a bit. Five. By the time he grows up, I hope he'll never have to use a gun."

"He's just a bit older than Alley Bear."

"And who's Alley Bear?"

"He's Ali Baha, really—my cousin. He belongs to Uncle Omar."

"So! The Arab side of your family, yes?"

I nodded, shot a glance at him sideways, and dared ask: "Why did you pick on us?"

"Us?"

"This—this place. It's mostly Uncle Omar's firm—his family's, I mean."

"Well. That is a complicated one. Maybe you wouldn't understand."

"I would!" I said indignantly. "I *can* understand things. Sometimes." I sighed.

He gave me a searching look. "I'm sure you can—but could I explain them to you? Do you know what 'representative' means?"

I had to admit that I didn't.

" 'Typical' ?"

Oh yes, I knew that. I said so.

"Well, then: first, this place is what we call a soft target— wide open to attack, and there was always a chance that we might net someone of influence or importance here." He smiled suddenly, looking pleased. "And perhaps we have this time... Then, your Uncle's firm is typical of many wealthy combines. An entire network—look at what it handles in these offices! Merchandise, chartering, but its side interests are more powerful, oil, banking, big important deals. They run like spider threads across the Middle East. Turkey, Greece, Iran, Arabia. And then on to India. And—to Israel. Do you see what all this means?"

I thought deeply. "It means that Uncle Omar has a lot of friends. Fa says that's a good thing."

"Yes, and what—Never mind. I said I wouldn't give you a political lecture. Anyway, we want his friends to act as our friends too. And we want the world to know what is suffered in places as far apart as Kurdistan and Palestine."

But I sensed condemnation, and I was bewildered, feeling I should be standing up for someone, not sure how. He wasn't Uncle Omar's friend, so whose friend was he? I was afraid he might be friends with what my mother called "anti-Christian Marxists—those dreadful people".

"Bear loves Uncle Omar."

"I'm sure he does. I think you like him too?"

"Oh yes. A lot." I sighed. "Uncle Omar has a photograph of Bear with my Aunt Sheikhah. It's in his pocket. Bear's photo is always there."

"I expect your father carries one of you too? It's a thing fathers do." He patted his own shirt pocket.

I didn't answer, and he didn't ask again. I was glad that the road drill started up just then, like before, but a little nearer. Arabi tightened his grip on the gun, the bones of his hand stuck out hard through the skin. The angles of his face stood out sharper, too. His whole body went taut. All at once he looked very much what he was: as dangerous as the gun.

My skin prickled. I was wondering if I could slip back to my chair unnoticed, when there was a great clatter of feet outside, and Yusuf and Yahia bundled Fa and Omar and some other hostages back into the room.

10 ARABI STOOD UP, and I escaped to Fa.

He was red in the face, his lips pressed tight together. That anger was something familiar, so I clutched his hand, and he held on absently. Uncle Omar was quiet as usual. Just to be near him made me feel better. Now and then he glanced at Fa in a question-mark way—I could see he had something on his mind.

"Only fools without any understanding would try deceiving us!" jeered Yahia.

"We understand you're illegally holding us. We've answered questions, we've done everything you tell us, and now you threaten us." Fa sounded icy and controlled. I was proud of him: a great marble statue, solid and strong.

Yahia swung round on Omar. "You thought to put it over on us, didn't you?" He shook his fist in Omar's face. I'd never seen that done before. The fist was tight-bunched, it might fly off at Omar if he wasn't careful. "Think again, then!" And Yusuf growled out in Arabic, "Death to Israeli lovers and other rotten arse-lickers—"

"*You* say we concealed Mr. Mizerachi's identity from you, and it's made you distrust us," said Omar. "You didn't ask us before—but now you know. Apart from that, surely the main thing is that they're near a solution outside? We must stay calm, and wait in peace with one another. Best if you keep us all together still, Mizerachi too. That will make for trust."

Suddenly I realised Mr. Bedrawi was still absent. Was *he* Mr. Mizerachi? The man my parents rowed so much about?

"Peace, trust! Words! No more words—we spit on them,

we spit on *you*. If they don't hear our words, perhaps they hear shooting, eh? Perhaps you'll understand *that* medicine when you take it—"

I had my arms round Fa's right leg in a tremendous grip. I don't think he even noticed. Arabi was standing well back, braced against the wall. He held his gun high, covering us.

There was some pushing going on, some shoving around. The African yelled out, "Stop! Stop this now." All at once there was a kind of scrum, people down on the floor, someone being shaken, guns cocked. I thought, This is it, we're all dead, and I shut my eyes tight and lost Fa's hand, and then I was down on the floor too, with someone sitting on me, and winded and whooping away like when I had whooping cough.

Funnily enough, it was my whooping that brought a kind of truce. The elephant sitting on me—that's how it felt—got off, and Yahia actually held me up while I caught my breath and lost it again, and then found it where it belonged. I was dusted down and put back in my chair, and Omar was sitting there beside me, and Fa was leaning against the wall, examining a thin trickle of scarlet on his hand.

"The West must learn we've right on our side." Arabi's voice—very calm and cool after the flare-up. "We're sorry for you, though concealing an Israeli's presence from us has not helped you, but it's our only way. All else has been tried—though even other Freedom Fighting groups knock our cause, squabbling between themselves. *We* stand for the truth." His voice might be cool, but those pulses leapt like anything in his neck and cheek.

"We're not responsible, we're sorry for anyone oppressed —anywhere in the world! But this is a matter for the United Nations. What can we do about it here? Nothing."

I think that's what one of the Directors said.

"You can be used for bargaining, that's all you're good for! And publicity. And if that's not enough, you can die, bastard

73

shits and sons of pigs that you are." This was Rashid, back again, prowling—a black panther with a smell under its nose. When his baleful glance reached me I felt shrivelled, sure he'd string me up by the neck with fewer qualms than if I were a one-too-many kitten.

The bouncy clerk yelped. The other Director said: "We demand you let us go," in a way that sounded soft and silly.

Rashid suddenly screamed, "If those friends of yours out there are also up to any funny tricks, you'll regret it. More time they keep asking for—what are they doing with it, eh? Making nooses for us? A little more and we shoot you one by one, and the Israeli will go first. They'll see we mean what we say. Let the whole world see! If they get inside this house they'll find a load of bloody corpses."

His shouting stopped as suddenly as it began. There was just that road-drilling outside, and a funny little whimper that I couldn't place till I found I was making it myself.

Uncle Omar said very quietly, "How can you act like this before a child? You'll end by alienating everyone."

(I didn't understand, then, what "alienating" meant—but I could guess by his tone.)

"And how will they hear of it?" asked Rashid, soft as silk. It froze my whimper on the spot.

They stared at each other. Neither blinked nor looked away.

"What has terrorism ever won, tell me that?" asked Omar at last, even quieter than before. "You think it creates justice —or more terror?"

"It draws attention to the wrongs of innocent people." Rashid sounded like a play, and bogus through and through. Even at my age I could see he was far from innocent himself, and I felt people wouldn't want to help him, and I knew I didn't. Then he suddenly changed his tune, and was desperate and sincere and quite human. "Can't you see what's happening to some Arab peoples—you, an Arab?

Surely you can understand why we act this way? Think of Kurdistan—of Palestine. All Arabs should be brothers."

He held out his arms. For a moment I thought he was going to hug Omar, and I hoped he wouldn't drop his grenade, specially as Omar was standing right beside me.

"Can't you see?" he repeated.

Omar just held out his hands palm upwards, in a gesture of despair. He said at last, "I can see . . . but people are less free than you imagine. Everywhere. And what is one man's justice is another's disaster. Solutions must be found—but true solutions come slowly, not by violence."

"The camps *are* violence! And what is done in Kurdistan—"

They went on arguing. I lost track, because I was watching Fa. He seemed very quiet, since they came back into the room. But of course they were using Arabic, anyway.

"Violence always boomerangs," put in the baldheaded old clerk quite mildly at last. "It won't help your 'innocents' to murder us."

"I wouldn't worry, if I were you," said Rashid. "You won't be here to know. And we shall start with the gentleman you so unwisely thought to protect." When he said that, he wore a wide, pleased grin.

Since I was only eight when I heard this and was scared stiff too, I may have fudged the argument somewhat, though the gist of it is right. And I think I've put down quite well how convinced both sides were of their own logic. It's what I've noticed about arguments, they can finish with smiles or blows, but whichever it is people mostly end up with their own views. I can make rings round my friends when I'm arguing, but I don't convince anyone, except, maybe, my cousin Ali Baha.

So far I'd kept the old Proust technique in reserve. I was saving the bitter-chocolate idea for the part that would be really hard to face. Already the amount of words flowing through my pen amazed me, and I hated MacArthur and Shirley for having got me into the grip of this awful thing. Now I had a compulsion to write it all down, even though I couldn't use the half of it. It was going to take me days to get it all out of my system, it even haunted me at home, or when I was out and about with my friends, doing other things...

I sat and doodled a bit, looking gloomily out of the window, and there was that great pouncer of a cat lying near the crocuses and sparrows with its eyes soulfully half-closed. It seemed so innocent: "I am a good sweet puzzy-wussy, I'm not what you think of me at all." I opened the window, slamming it up so violently that it scattered the sparrows, and the cat looked daggerpoints at me—a "damn you, you've spoilt my game" look.

I closed the window, thinking of the mean deceptions that animals and people use. People are a dab hand at it. Both with other people and themselves. It was something I learned a lot about, the hard way, on Days Three and Four.

11 DAY THREE HAD begun badly with Rashid's threats; but the flare-up between terrorists and hostages died down as suddenly as it began, and the gunmen trooped from the room, leaving behind the large silent man they called Miqrim, who had guarded the women's room on Day One.

I was sure now that Mr. Mizerachi must be Mr. Bedrawi —who was still the only absent person. *Had* Fa known he would be here today? I longed to ask him, but he was so silent. I stole sidelong glances at him. His expression was extra-lofty, almost injured. I couldn't make it out. It seemed the wrong look for what was happening—we might all be on a plane, or dead, by nightfall. Omar, I saw, was watching him too.

Once or twice before I'd seen Fa look like that. The last time had been when our new neighbour in the flat above kept nipping in and out to bring me and Alley Bear sweets. Sweets were bad for our teeth, but I couldn't see why they were suddenly so specially bad that my mother threw a pot plant at Fa, and screamed all up and down the hall that it was too much, and she wasn't having it here wherever else it might be going on (and I didn't make proper sense of that till some years later). It was all the more puzzling to see him wear this look when there were no neighbours with long fair hair and chocolates, but only some desperate women hostages in another room, who hadn't tried to slip me anything during the short while I was with them, not even one boiled sweet.

And it was a puzzling day in general, very edgy. Even Arabi's face was tight-set and secretive. He didn't speak to us,

77

simply acted as though we weren't there—or as though he couldn't bear to know we were. My stomach had churned so often now that it stopped reacting, and I just felt this was some strange dream, extended far beyond a dream's usual waking point. The African, too, looked as if he was in a trance. He spent most of his time leaning back against the wall, rocking slightly, his hands clasped around his knees. His blue and yellow robe flowed about him. With half-shut eyes he stared dreamily into its folds—and I stared too, seeing black-brown bodies twirling between yellow sand and deep blue waves, lost people, people no one helped...I looked away.

Midday brought food. Arabi doled it out in half-empty plastic boxes—slap down on our knees, whether we wanted it or not. But he gave me mine quite gently, saying, "All right, Mr. Zed?" before he turned away, not waiting for reply.

Mr. Zed. I liked that. It sounded strange, but friendly.

The bouncy clerk—who cried in the night—shoved his food aside, and sat with his head down on his knees, talking to himself. It wasn't awfully pleasant, in fact it made me downright uneasy. I could tell it was getting at Miqrim too, which was worse. So I just kept thinking hard about my new name, Mr. Zed. And what Arabi was thinking of, his Feisal perhaps, who wasn't much older than Bear. Did Arabi call him "Mr. Feisal" sometimes? I guessed he felt about him as Omar felt about Bear. How horrid that Arabi and Omar were both shut in here feeling bad in the same way! Still, it wasn't Omar's fault, it was Arabi's...or, at least, Rashid's.

Abruptly Fa spoke over my head to Omar, as if he were continuing a conversation, although they hadn't spoken directly to one another since coming back into the room. "I know they checked everyone's name to start with, but they would have found out sooner or later. They might have looked through your secretary's appointment book, for instance. They would have checked that sort of thing eventually, even if they hadn't grown suspicious. You heard them say that Karim's radio had picked up something about there being an Israeli here."

Omar shrugged, and went on eating.

"Omar," said Fa appealingly, in a worried voice.

When Uncle Omar simply went on eating, Fa shoved his own foodbox aside as the clerk had done.

At last Omar muttered, "They didn't look. That fellow Rashid was only following a hunch, after what they heard. You should have denied all knowledge of him."

"What good would that have done? Lying might have blown things up entirely, later on—given them cause to take it out on Thomas. They don't seem to bother about children."

I couldn't make head or tail of this, but I felt warm inside at the way Fa was protecting me.

"—and there's no point in being roughed up for something that several people in this room knew already," said Fa, very dignified, all marble.

Omar stopped eating, and said, "Now he'll be the first. You heard them."

"Nonsense, it's all bluff. He's not all that important, either. You know things are going well, they're talking—they'll get us out."

Fa had raised his voice on the last words. The clerk stared at us and began shouting, "What's going on outside? Those bastards! They'd act fast enough to save their own rotten hides—callous stonewalling sods!" He started shaking his head about and moaning in an awful way.

I dropped my box, and bits of food went rolling about the floor. No one noticed, because Yahia had come rushing into the room, gun cocked, and Miqrim was already at the clerk's side trying to shake him into silence, so that what with that and the shaking of his head he was flopping about all over the place like a hooked and landed fish.

He was quiet at last, with a sort of glazed glare that was worse than his moanings. When Yahia had left and Miqrim was back on guard I slipped off my chair to collect my food. There was one big fat bit of cheese, green and grainy, and I gave it to the clerk, hoping it would unglaze him; pushing it into his hand and closing his fingers round it.

Tears began to ooze from his eyes again, which looked enormous, all black and watery.

"It's all right," I said hurriedly, rather offhand. "I don't want it, you can eat it," and I went back to my perch before he could get upset. If there was crying to be done, I could do it myself. It wasn't very nice cheese, anyhow.

Fa and Omar were still arguing.

"—they would have got round to *you* soon, and then we should have seen." Fa sounded sarcastic, and as though he was almost hating Omar, though I couldn't for the life of me imagine why. Omar saw me listening, and clamped his mouth shut in angry folds. Through their silence I could sense unspoken words buzzing to and fro over my intervening self with the speed and flair of ping-pong balls, zzz, snp.

I began to get that gloomy feeling you have when people won't talk just because you're there. Peering from the corner of one eye I could see Fa's hands clasped tight around his knees, and peering from the other I saw Omar's cheeks drawn in hollow, as if sucking something he didn't like.

I thought, It's all the fault of that Mr. Mizerachi again, there's always trouble about him somehow. I couldn't actually remember Uncle Omar ever telling Fa that he'd be here to lunch with us on that first day—but perhaps he wouldn't say so before my mother . . .

Just then Rashid appeared looking blacker and bristlier than ever, with Cheetah. They were nattering away at top speed until Rashid broke off to tell Miqrim, "That security guard's worse. It must be why they're holding off—we don't believe we'll get that plane."

"The English police say so?" Miqrim scowled.

"Foreign broadcast—Karim's long-wave radio picked it up. The English say nothing, it must have leaked out," said Rashid. "From now on we can forget about any form of trust. The boy stays too, for one thing. I'm glad we didn't free him."

They exchanged looks. There were some things they didn't need to say. I suppose there were only three people in the room who couldn't understand that something else had happened—Fa, Señor Juan and the African. No, four—because the clerk had lost touch completely and was staring straight ahead of him, mumbling, and rolling my bit of cheese about between his fingers like the Lean Man's worry beads.

"So! We can step up the pressure all round." Cheetah looked at me, and laughed. He looked at Fa and made a sort of jeery noise, deep in his throat. I got the feeling that he didn't like the English and did like taunting Fa, who got the message and flushed all over his face. Of course, apart from the jeery noise he hadn't understood what they were on about. It was Omar who stood up all in one quick movement, to say, "But you must let the child go. You must."

"Omar—what is it? What's happened?"

"Be quiet, can't you? Keep your damn fool mouth shut this time."

I expected Fa to snarl back at Omar, but all he did was lean across to press his hand on my shoulder, weightily—meaning, we really belonged to one another, not to anyone else. He meant that, I do believe it: it's what he was feeling then. I had this odd sense of sureness, and when that happens with me it's usually bang on, like hitting the bullseye when there seems to be a line stretched straight from your eye to the centre of the dartboard.

The gunmen stared at Omar as though he wasn't there.

"Meet our demands, or—? And start with Mizerachi?" muttered Rashid, and Cheetah nodded. Miqrim didn't seem to have much say in anything.

"Thomas—what's going on, Thomas?" whispered Fa urgently.

This time it was Cheetah who shut him up. He and Rashid prowled up and down in front of us, glaring, as tense and nervy as they were early on Day One. Omar didn't sit again, he stayed absolutely still. We all knew we mustn't move then, we were a trigger's-breadth from disaster, from the fierce flowering of that lemon-shape in Cheetah's left hand.

12 IN THE END Rashid turned on his heel and strode out, walking heavily and fast with a decisive air. We waited. Even the clerk was silent. Distant orders echoed round the staircase well, followed by scuffling and sounds like something—someone—being dragged.

A voice cried out, weak and lost. I knew whose: Mr. Mizerachi's. There was further scuffling, a thud, a kind of protesting yelp. We heard one of the terrorists laughing. Then silence.

Cheetah broke it. You could tell he was grinning, even though he was muffled to the eyes. He spoke direct to Fa, in English: "They tie him, poor Mr. Mizerachi. Ready." He held up his grenade, and made a throwing movement, and laughed.

"Ay-ah!" moaned the Spaniard. "*Ave Maria, gratiae plena*—

Fa's hand on my shoulder jerked, just like a dog's leg kicks in sleep. On my other side Omar let out a long sigh. I felt cold through and through: the chill of snow when it comes right over the tops of your wellies, drenching your feet in ice water.

That afternoon dragged nastily. I kept thinking how much worse it must be dragging for poor Mr. Mizerachi, tied up and waiting, a kind of scapegoat. It didn't seem possible that people could do such things—not near the friendly Park with its crocuses coming out, and dogs running and barking on the grass.

It was four o'clock by the golden face of Omar's watch when Rashid and Yahia came rushing in again, excited, almost jubilant. I was scared for a moment that they would slap Cheetah on the back and explode his lemon.

"We have a plane, and—"

"Yes! They give in!"

"A plane—when? *And* what of our demands?" Cold water from Cheetah.

"It takes time, naturally! Some hours, tomorrow, maybe early, and—"

"And maybe not. Maybe more funny tricks, and to hell with us all, eh? Shoot him, now. Put an end to this. Let them see we're in earnest."

"*No.* Now we're succeeding we can take these—" Rashid jerked his head at us— "out with us. Then they will bargain, how they will! If we shoot that Israeli shit now, we lose a card."

"Shoot him! They're playing with us. Open their eyes." Cheetah lowered his gun and for the first time unmuffled his face, tearing his kuffieh aside. An old reddish-blue scar puckered up half his chin, scored deep into the flesh—it could have been mauled by a wild animal. He pointed at it with his grenade hand. "*This* opened mine."

Rashid's jollity vanished. Questions and answers came too fast in their different dialects for me to catch them. The gunmen's quarrel sprang up fierce as a sea-squall covering an already choppy sea. Quite suddenly Rashid actually hit Cheetah, who reeled backward with a terrifying snarl. His left hand swung up. I gasped, watching his finger on the pin. His lips were drawn back, almost grinning. Deliberately, he held up his grenade: against everyone.

Seconds were ticking us away. Across my mind ran big fiery letters: God's punishment. Was it all because I'd stolen some of Bear's egg, as well as eating my own—the one that came up in the road? That was greed *and* theft in one. Sometimes my family had made me feel the smallest thing I did wrong could bring down the heavens. Now it had, or was going to—

But seconds passed, the arm fell, the grenade was still there

84

in Cheetah's hand. He said, sort of growling it out through his teeth, "*Fools*... that guard's badly sick—and you think we have a plane?"

"He mayn't be so bad, after all... besides, the Brits are tough as anyone, what's one guard to them against—" another jerk of the head at us—"all of these?"

Cheetah shook his head gloomily. There was a pause while they all looked at one another. Just then the road drill started up again, going in short sharp bursts.

Cheetah said, "*Huh*—hear that. I don't like it."

They listened, fingering their guns. At last Rashid shrugged. "Maybe... but that road was being dug, when we got in."

"Couldn't carry so far. It's nearer—and they had no drills, then." They were both speaking slowly, weighing things. I had no difficulty in following them now.

"That sound does carry on warm air," put in Yahia.

Rashid shrugged again—but so wearily. "Trust... not trust. Getting jumpy is a danger, but—you know that we agreed on peaceful protest, *if* we got a plane..." But he sounded uncertain when he added, "Nothing has changed."

"*I* have changed! My mind's changed. We should be willing martyrs for the Arab people—our people. And we should take some of these with us." Cheetah glared straight at me, and I thought of the Old Testament and human sacrifices and wicked Baal who liked children best. There was Herod too. Being small didn't always help.

"Well... we'll vote on it, then." Rashid sounded unlike their leader now, just tired, and as if anyone could push him around. I didn't see how they voted—but it seemed that Miqrim sided with Cheetah, and Yahia with Rashid.

"I'll see what Karim, Arabi and Yusuf think," said Rashid still more wearily. "That will decide it."

"You go too," Cheetah told Miqrim. "I want to know what's said."

Rashid looked insulted. Yet he said nothing, just went out with Yahia, Miqrim trailing them. I didn't like that. It was definitely Cheetah's triumph. There were two leaders now, with two teams. When the siege started Rashid would have barked him down. By this time, though, we'd been dead, not dead, so often, that my legs didn't even quiver. It was growing to be a game of pulling petals off a flower, he kills me, he kills me not. I just stared at Fa, and wondered how we'd go. Blown up, or—

This time the petals still fell right. When Rashid returned it was plain the leadership had shifted back on to his shoulders. He came with an easy lope, and a cocky bristling of his black moustache. Karim followed, pushing Mr. Mizerachi ahead of him. Karim was very fair, with a scarred cheek. He looked rather Swedish or German—perhaps he was a mix, like me.

The Cheetah didn't even ask for the result, he just let out an exasperated grunt, and wound his kuffieh ends up tight around his face again. Wounded angry Cheetah, going into hiding.

Poor Mr. Mizerachi looked in a very bad way. His bland surface had quite gone, and his glasses were broken, and balanced unevenly on his nose. In just that long afternoon of being tied he'd grown into an old, old man, saggy in face and body, scuffed and dirty and not at all as if he'd flick a napkin at anyone. He crept across the room, avoiding our eyes. One of his wrists had wire around it, twisted like barbed wire. He must have struggled, because both his wrists were sore and red. He tottered to his old place, stood facing the wall, and then sank down slowly to his shaky knees. He knelt like that quite a while. At first I thought he was praying, but he was crying—or perhaps he was doing both. The gunmen were watching him, and I could tell that even they were sorry for him. Except, maybe, Cheetah. You couldn't see what he was thinking, muffled up like that, yet his eyes never altered, except to change from mad and red to mad and yellow, according to the light.

You might think that some other hostages near Mr. Mizerachi would have tried to comfort him, but it really seemed as if the gunmen were sorrier than they were. They couldn't draw away, exactly, but they gave him guarded guilty looks under lowered lids—very like the way people at school behaved when someone was singled out and punished for something everyone had a hand in. Butter wouldn't melt in *your* mouths, would it? our teachers used to say, when we looked like that.

Mr. Mizerachi raised his head at last, and turned towards us. A bit of sag had gone, and he shot words very harsh and quick at us in bad English—so fast and in so strong a guttural accent that I didn't get it. I don't know if Fa did. Anyway, he didn't answer, just stared straight ahead while a faint colour rose up his neck under his prickly fair beard. Omar acted quite unaware. He was lying on his back, stretched out as comfortably as possible on some cushions, feet towards the door, head towards me, arms folded across his chest.

Looking down on him, I could see a curve of lip and moulded chin, the wing-sweep of his eyebrows, his heavy lids' half-moon shape beneath them, then his nose foreshortened and a curve of calmer moustache than Rashid's, not embattled-looking or bristled but a silky one. Alley Bear used to stroke and stroke it, saying, "Pet dog, pet dog," and then bubble with laughter and pull until Omar squeaked with pretended pain, and threatened him with terrible tossings to the ceiling.

I remember that I guessed he had withdrawn from our surroundings. On our room's ceiling he was seeing, not circles of harsh light and shade thrown up by the rigged lamp, but the plump round faces of Sheikhah and Alley Bear. As I watched, his right hand went fumblingly to his breast pocket, and he pulled out his photograph of Bear and cupped it in his hand, and lay looking at it, and to my dismay I saw two fat teardrops well from the corners of his eyes and crawl slowly down his face.

13

IT WAS ONE of the things about Day Three that I least wanted to remember. I sat staring out at the patch of green again—now dark inky-blue green, since the light was fading fast. Cat and sparrows had gone. There was less and less school noise—just an occasional voice high and clear as someone shouted goodnight to someone else, or a door slammed, or footsteps went down the passage from the gym while a confident whistle dwindled away into silence. It wouldn't be long before George Shirley or someone would be round to lock up and ask how I was getting on.

The pile of paper at my right hand was growing steadily. Since it was dusk already, I decided to jettison the rest of Day Three, which was stalemate anyway, and pitch in again with my thoughts later on that same night, when I was lying there remembering how only four nights earlier I'd been safe in my own bedroom, hearing the friendly tick of my Swiss wall clock—its pinecone pendulum beating to and fro—and a deep murmur of sound from Fa's library, and the higher one of women's voices from the drawing room. My mother and Aunt Sheikhah were probably drinking coffee, with a touch of rosewater or orange-flavoured in the Lebanese fashion. In this, as in many other small things, my mother stuck to the customs of her family.

Next door Bear was wakeful too, crooning aloud some story about his special bed-companion, a stuffed donkey. My mother had given it to him, and he had named it Mustafa.

"And then—and then—and then—" in a rising Arabic chant—"Mustafa Donkey met a—a Fatima Donkey..."

89

Down the passage a door opened. The deep murmur in the library had stopped.

"And after that Mustafa and Fatima went up a tree," shouting—"They met a cow, and—and—"

"And then they turned over and went to sleep, a deep deep sleep till morning—" said Omar's voice.

Bear gave a whoop of delight. It was what he'd been working for, of course. *I* used to work for that sort of thing, without success. My clock ticked to and fro; friendly, but not personal. I lay on my back, feet together, arms behind my head, staring at my shut door. It was visible because Aunt Sheikhah had guessed my fear of the dark, and had bought me a wainscot lamp—a small round dim moon, that plugged straight in at wainscot level. Because it was a gift I was allowed to keep it, and even have it on at weekends. Actually, I lit it each night, and had schooled myself to wake at dawn and nip out of bed to turn it off.

Bear and Omar were enjoying a chat-up next door. I strained my ears but could hear nothing, except a sort of happy treble sound like muffled birdsong, and a lower rumbling one. Then it was the rumble alone, at fewer and fewer intervals, and I guessed that Bear was falling asleep. At last his door opened softly. I counted three, and coughed as loudly as I dared.

Omar's footsteps stopped outside my door. I coughed again.

"Thomas?" My door opened. "Why are you awake too?"

"Got a cough."

"Ah." There was a smile in Omar's voice. He walked into the room, and sat down on my bed.

"Not a bad cough," I said defensively. "Just a very little one."

"A very sudden little one."

I stopped playing that game. "It wasn't really there at all."

"What about a drink of water for the cough that wasn't?"

There was a handbasin in my room, and he filled my tooth-mug and brought it over to me. I didn't really want it, but I drank slowly, spinning out the moment, and feeling light and happy. Omar had only been with us a few days, yet I felt he'd been here always.

"Aren't you cold, with that window so wide open?"

"No, I like it—it smells nice, what's coming in." The flat looked out over gardens, and London's fumy smell was overlaid by scents of damp earth and sappy spring.

"We sleep with ours shut." He took the mug from me. "We're unused to this climate," and he shivered.

"Must be a goose walking over your grave," I told him.

"What?" He sounded startled.

"It's what people say here when you shiver: 'There's a goose—'"

"Oh! Well, I hope mine's in a warmer place than this. Now cover up, Thomas—that's right, arms and all." He bent to tuck me in, and kissed me on the forehead. "Ali Baha is asleep—you should be too."

He went away, casting a glance at my wainscot moon, and somehow managing not to shut the door quite tightly. I heard Fa's voice boom out along the corridor: "What's going on there—has Thomas been keeping your kid awake?"

"The other way around."

The library door was closed then, shutting off their talk.

So that's what I was thinking of, late at night on Day Three. After a while I began to shift around so restlessly that Yusuf took pity on me, and brought me a furry rug to lie on, by Omar's cushions. Fa moved across into my chair, breathing heavily. I don't know if he'd slept at all. Most of us had been slightly easier since Cheetah was relieved of duty. The gunmen holed up somewhere else to sleep, naturally they didn't tell us where.

It was Yusuf and Yahia who were guarding us that night,

dividing the watch. One or other catnapped by turn, but you felt they had one eye open, so to speak. They were jumpier after dark—I suppose it was the most likely time for attack—and very silent. None of us, prisoners or guards, liked the bouts of mumbling from the clerk, who rocked and rocked, arms clasped around his knees, but we'd grown used to it, like the Lean Man's worrybeads, the Spaniard's rosary, and people's bottoms uppermost in regular Muslim prayer.

I was just wishing resentfully that the smelly fug in here could be replaced by the sappy evening garden smells outside our flat, when light alert footsteps heralded Arabi's arrival. He looked almost electric with excitement. The rigged light caught his eyes' brilliant gleam, the shine on his gun. His voice fairly rang across the shadowy room, jerking everyone awake. "It's true! We have the plane. Before noon tomorrow. And the bus to take us there. A letter through the box. It came."

He repeated it in English.

Yusuf was all smiles, and Yahia jumped down from the desk where he was sitting. The rest of us sat, or lay, like stone. Except the clerk.

"But our friends—in Kurdistan—in—?"

"For negotiation still—when we reach Libya. With these."

His hand swept out towards us.

The plane.

So all this was going on and on. Perhaps we'd come down in the Libyan desert, be stuck in that plane, a more cramped, hot and hateful prison than this room. And easier to destroy. I gulped and reached for Omar's hand. But he had pulled himself up on to his elbows, and was saying fiercely, "The boy?—the women? You won't take them out there, *surely*."

Arabi just looked at him, his mouth quirking up in a half smile. "You argue that with Rashid. We'll certainly leave *him*—" He pointed at the swaying, mumbling clerk. "Perhaps the boy too—" And then he spoke straight to me:

"But if not—A great adventure, eh, Mr. Zed? To tell your friends about." And he left the room before Fa or Omar could start arguing. He was so cocksure. His confident walk told me, more than his words, that they had won, hands down. Nobody, I'm sure, neither guards nor prisoners, slept much that night.

14 THERE WASN'T TIME to read it through, but I was pretty sure everything of importance about Day Three was there. I stuffed the papers into their folder, and was just locking up the drawer when George Shirley appeared.

"Time to go home. How's the great work coming along?"

"Better," I said. Offhand.

"Finished that chocolate yet?"

"Only licked it, so far."

His eyebrows shot up, a look of gentle mockery. "What will it end as, Zed—a three-volume novel?"

"Well—Proust comes in thirteen." (I'd looked up Proust, Marcel, in the school library's biographical dictionary, since George S. first offered me the chocolate.)

He gave me the kind of piercing glance that masters pull out when they've been friendly yet don't expect you to be too equal back. "If you let it drag on into the summer term, it won't get you off practice at the nets, you know."

Cricket is compulsory at Consort's, whether you prefer tennis or not. Old George has probably heard me saying that all this jockeying about in coaches to the ground at Twickenham is a non-event.

I sighed meaningly. "Oh well—if there's no time to finish, then there isn't." I looked at him deadpan, trying to project a vision of the School Centenary Number's empty pages into his mind. He gave me a hard shrewd stare in return.

"Just how far along are you, Zed?"

"About two-thirds, I should think. But I'll have to hone it down enormously, there's far too much."

He grunted. "So I should think. Cut along home, now. And keep that cricket bat oiled."

"If there's time—*sir*," I replied, and was outside the room before he could start thinking of abstract concepts like respect. All my friends had gone home by this time, or were busy elsewhere. It was almost dark outside, and my bus was coming and I had to run for it. I went up top, to sit on the front seat. It was swaying like a crow's nest, but I enjoyed that, had it to myself, and sat looking down on the black road speeding backward. The thought of delving into Day Four was making me low-spirited. I cursed MacArthur and Shirley. This probing the past isn't all the shrinks say it is.

"That's your home stop you asked for, back there," said the conductor. at my elbow. (We often travel on the same bus.)

"Okay. I'm not getting off there after all," I told him, digging in my pocket for more coins. (It's daylight robbery.) "I've changed my mind."

"Just don't try that again," he said, giving me the second ticket. "The Inspector doesn't like it."

I didn't argue It wouldn't have convinced him, though my change of mind was genuine.

It was only a short walk at the other end, and then there was the block of flats: thinnish and high-rise—a bit bleak, I always thought it. The lift shot me up to the fifth floor, and I pinged the bell and waited. Aunt Sheikhah herself opened the front door. Her round face is a bit more crumpled than it used to be, but a nice crumple, soft. It always makes me think of garden pansies—not the sort of thing you say aloud. It was looking serious and rather worried, but when she found me outside it changed to warm and pleased.

"Oh, it is you, Zed! Come in." She nearly always speaks English these days, it's to encourage Alley B., who's sometimes lazy and has to keep at it in his school.

"I'm not stopping long—I was passing, so I just looked in to see Alley B."

"Passing? Yes, of course," she said. Aunt Sheikhah's never tiresome about questions. She was looking vaguely at her bag, on the hall table. "Fares are so expensive, Zed." She took out 50p and slipped it in my pocket, although I tried to stop her.

"He is in his room," she said, over her shoulder, as she tripped down the passage ahead of me. "He will not come out. He has a—" She paused and stared hard at a flower painting on the wall—it might have been quite new to her. She sighed. "It's that new set he's been placed in, at his school," she murmured, almost to herself. "I do not know if Ali will want to talk, but . . . Anyway, there is still some tea, if you would like it."

Although it was so late the thought of more tea wasn't bad at all. Even though it was more likely to be synthetic coffee.

"Shall I just look in on him first?" I didn't wait, but headed off down the corridor and tapped on his door. There was no reply.

"Hi—Bear! It's me, Zed. Can I come in?"

Still no reply. Just a hurried scrambling sound, like someone getting off a bed. I opened the door very slowly, to give him time, and slipped inside and shut it again behind me. He was over by the window, looking out. The shape of his head was outlined against the evening sky where Hammersmith lights made a coppery glow beyond the opposite houses. A very modern, dramatic, London sort of view I always thought it. I've always liked that kind of thing. Exciting. Just as the terrific height, the terrifying bankless zigzag roads, the mimosa, the orchards and the juniper smells of the Christian Mountain used to excite me a different way when I was a little kid sitting on my grandfather's knee . . .

"Shall I switch the light on?"

This time I didn't wait for his reply. Light spilled out from the wall and ceiling strips, and the window-panes turned thick dark blue, losing the coppery sky completely.

He turned round at last to face me, and although he was so much younger than I we were almost on a level. He had a hand up as though to shield his eyes, and specially the left side of his face, but I could see that he'd been crying. When he lowered the hand, reluctantly, there was a beauty of a black eye. His round face was still ridiculously like Sheikhah's, with a touch of Omar's thrown in. He glared at me accusingly from the eye that wasn't shut, almost as if I'd given him the blow myself, and walked past to throw himself face downward on the bed.

"Oh, come on," I said. "It's not as bad as that."

I went over to the wooden shelf where he kept his model aircraft. There was an array of brushes, adhesives, and a scale model of a Spitfire still in its undercoat, beautifully made. I picked it up and had a tactful squint at it, while all the time Bear lay sniffing and gulping on the bed.

"You'll make it worse, crying like that," I said at last. "People say use raw steak, that's the thing." There was some in our freezer. Pity I didn't have it with me.

"When are you going to finish this?" I touched the model, realised he didn't know what I was touching, and added, "Spitfire."

He wiped his nose heavily on the back of his hand, or that was what it sounded like. "Can't even see it, can I? It's—it was for my project, and it won't be done in time. I'll get bad marks for that, and more bad marks for fighting. It's the third time he's gone for my face where it shows, filthy beast."

"Cliff again? Didn't anyone else see him? Did you get him too?"

He sat up, then. Shaking his head dolefully as though it was still spinning from the blow. He felt his eye, with a tender touch.

"You'll have to get him, you know. Anyway, once. Or it

97

will just go on and on." He began to sniff again, and I could see it was his worst fear. I looked away—at the models, at the childish piggybank on the chest of drawers. He'd had it right back in the old days at our flat. It came from Switzerland like my now defunct Swiss clock. "*Spar Schweine*" ran the Gothic lettering on the pig's bulging flank. Savings pig. Alley B. might be no natural fighter, but he was very determined. He'd saved a long while for his toolkit, and an even longer one for his cassette player. He was bound to be saving now for something. I edged Aunt Sheikhah's 50p from my pocket, and dropped it in. It made a slight ringing sound. I cleared my throat too late.

Bear slewed round on the bed.

"Did you drop something in my bank?"

"Two wretched p," I said carelessly. "Filthy bus change. What started it this time, anyway?"

He got up, to sit with his legs dangling over the side of the bed. The eye was worse, swelling rapidly. "It hurts, *how* it does." He palmed it with his right hand, and squinted round it at me. "It was nothing *I* did. He came up to me seeming quite different, friendly almost, so I thought it was all right and smiled, and he said, 'Don't you get that grin on your ugly mug when you look at me'—and pushed and punched me——an' ran."

"Don't you ever learn?" I asked. "It's a tough world out there—not everyone in it wants to be your friend."

"But I like people—I want them to like me."

"Practise fighting with your friends. Let people like Cliff know you can defend yourself. It's the only way."

"My friends aren't like that, Zed. They don't like fighting, either."

I walked about the room a bit. "Look," I said at last, "you fight me. You fight me hard, and I'll show you what to do. When you've learned to win, you can take the others on."

"Oh, don't be silly—I don't want to fight you."

"You must."

"I won't. I can't really see you, anyway."

There was nothing else for it. I picked up the Spitfire and hurled it at the opposite wall, where it splintered into fragments. Three weeks' work and another bad mark . . . Alley B. howled an animal howl of sheer fury, and leapt from the bed.

I reached the door first and wrenched it open, though his fists were flailing at my shoulders. Laughing, I fled down the corridor, though not too fast for his one-eyed pursuit, and he came behind me like a charging elephant, making an amazing noise. Where the passage widened into alcove I changed gear, wheeled, and put my hands up, dancing in front of him. He hesitated and I yelled, "Come on—that's what you do, see?" as I flicked him on the breastbone. He was whirling his arms, windmill fashion, and the flower painting came off the wall.

We went to and fro over it, with a sound of breaking glass, me showing him by example how to move his arms, and once kicking his right leg back into place for him, and all the time not really touching him to hurt but making him madder than a load of hornets, with that Spitfire on his mind already. Suddenly I slipped on the glass and opened up my guard, and he bunched his fist and came in fair and square, just as he should have done with the abominable Cliff, hitting me hard and accurately on the nose. If I could have spoken then I might have said: "See?" But I was speechless—it was a triumph, but a painful one.

Aunt Sheikhah came out of her sitting room a moment later, saying, "What in the name of Allah was all that noise about? And what has happened to my painting—" but stopped when she saw me standing there, bleeding from my rapidly swelling nose which already felt like a cucumber.

"Not you, too, Zed! Take him to the bathroom and pour cold water on his nose, Ali."

"I'm sorry," I said, as distinctly as I could. "I banged it on your painting when it came off the wall."

Both Alley B. and I were suddenly laughing crazily in spite of eyes and noses.

"You'd better stay to dine with us, and have a rest—I'll ring your mother, Zed." Sheikhah was trying to look severe and failing, she couldn't hide that she was actually more cheerful too. She didn't ask any more questions, and said no more about the picture, except to make Bear sweep up the glass.

That evening was quite a good one, after all. In the thrill of having done such damage, even if it was only to me, Alley Bear forgot to worry about bad marks or even the ruin of his project. The threat of Cliff had receded, now he was hopeful of giving him a swollen nose like mine. I was still doubtful about his chances in battle, though, and left begging him to avoid the windmill approach which could only lay him wide open to the Cliffs of this world.

"Come over on Saturday," I told him as I left, "and I'll show you a bit more—and 'ware Cliff until you've got it straight."

On the bus going home I began wondering what had made me think of going to Aunt Sheikhah's flat just then. Not that I didn't go there often, but not usually in the middle of the week, and after school. Telepathy, maybe—because there's always been a bond between Alley B. and me. Or had it all stemmed from my depression, my general sense of responsibility? On the whole, I decided, it was somehow tied up with all my delving back into Day Three, and the tears I'd seen on Uncle Omar's face. And Day Four was still hanging over me like a towering thundercloud.

"Oh, it's you again," said the same conductor as he took my fare. He peered at my nose, and grinned sourly. "Can't keep out of trouble this evening, can you? See you match the ticket to the home stop this time, mate—or you might find yourself in a spot more trouble."

As might have been expected, MacArthur was acid about

my clownish appearance next day in class. Soon I pulled out a large handkerchief and managed to milk my nose of another little bleed, in the hope that he'd take pity on me and send me home. All he did was let me off class for the whole afternoon.

"Thanks, sir," I said—maybe too eagerly: there was a very good film on at the Cinecenta, and I thought of taking my nose to it for a treat.

"And that will give you the chance to go ahead with your project, and still get off home at a reasonable hour."

No more "Thanks, sir," for bloody MacArthur. There's always a sting in the tail.

After lunchtime—as leisurely as I could make it—I went over to the study. My nose was swelling again after its enforced bleed, so I nursed it tenderly with my left hand while I spread out my papers. Then I took a bite of bitter chocolate, and settled down to wade straight into Day Four.

15 I WOKE ALMOST stifled by the usual fug, but it was an outburst of noise in the corridor that had roused me: the terrorists were shouting at each other. I couldn't get what it was all about, since the row was broken by bursts of competition from the road drill that had started up even closer and louder than before.

Omar had been roused too, and was sitting up beside me. Over my head he exchanged looks with Fa, and rose cautiously to his feet, unnoticed by Yahia and Yusuf who were over by the door, peering out. Anyone armed could have taken them unawares.

I whispered: "*Fa*—"

"Hush, Thomas—a moment."

There was a chorus of "What's going on?" and "What is it?" mainly in Arabic, of course. Señor Juan let out a volley of Spanish or Latin prayer. The Lean Man's worry beads broke, and went rolling away all over the floor.

Then the drilling stopped, and we heard one gunman yelling, "It's all a bloody trap," which made me horribly sure we were all for it any moment now. I cowered against Uncle Omar. For once he didn't notice; because just then the door was slapped wide open, making our guards jump hurriedly aside, and Rashid and Miqrim stormed into the room. Rashid advanced on Fa and started shouting Arabic into his face, forgetting that he couldn't understand—and I couldn't either, he was raving so, almost frothing at the mouth. In the distance the women could be heard screaming, little sharp shrieks like parrots.

Rashid suddenly turned to the Cats, and he was saying:

"Long-wave radio . . . picked it up," and "security guard" and "dirty trickery." Then he shouted it all out again to the room at large, in his bad English.

There was a silence. Worse than any before.

I felt Omar take a decision. (And perhaps I really did feel it, when I think of what MacArthur tells us in class now about up-to-date experiments to prove that thoughts have substance.) Anyway, before he stepped forward, I knew he was going to. It drew a wolfpack of eyes on to him.

"Please—" he sounded completely unafraid and in control—"Please, we haven't heard what this is all about—won't someone tell us?"

They looked taken aback. His walking forward like that and speaking so politely somehow calmed them down.

Rashid answered him. His eyes were staring and glistening. I didn't like the look of them at all. I thought that men who were going into battle probably looked like that.

"We'll put up with it no more." He spat it out at Omar between great pants—what with that and the staring and glistening I thought he looked like a mad dog, much worse than a battle-hungry soldier.

"But with what? We do not understand," repeated Omar, still very polite and patient.

"On relay—from North Africa—we hear it's all a lie—there is no plane arranged, no bus—and these promises are all a dirty British trick to wear us out and get more time."

I glanced at Fa, who was still sitting slumped in my armchair. I couldn't tell what he was thinking, or how much he guessed.

Beyond the Spaniard, Mr. Mizerachi was kneeling with his head down, as if he might crumple up at any moment.

"All this is mere whipped-up foreign rumour, isn't it?" said Omar very reasonably. "Has there been anything nearer home, here on British radio, that could make you doubt?"

Rashid looked uncertain.

But the moment slipped away from Omar, because just then the Cheetah came into the room, and Rashid was turning towards him almost submissively, and was saying, "You were right all along—you *are* right: settle accounts with one of them now", and the Cheetah looked all mad and red-eyed, and nodded his muffled head in Mr. Mizerachi's direction, and said: "Let's take that damned Israeli again—make a job of it." Mr. Mizerachi just gave a choked sort of sound, and toppled forward on his face and lay quite still.

"You can't shoot an unconscious man," said Omar, very white: always everyone's spokesman. "That would be dirty, shameful. Without honour." He sounded so dignified.

"Honour!" snapped the Cheetah. "Power politics threw out 'honour' long ago." He looked the three of us up and down as though he specially disliked us. "Once we start shooting, we'll go on—we'll show these English shits. We'll shoot one of you every twenty minutes till we get our way. The Israeli can go second, if you like. Since you're so keen on 'honour'—" he glared at Omar—"the rest of you can draw lots, except for second place. That gives you all a chance of 'honourable' martyrdom." He nodded at Yusuf: "Tell the others what's decided. And keep a very careful watch."

Yusuf hurried out. It was too clear that power had shifted right away from Rashid. I barely heard Omar explaining things to Fa, I was too busy praying and praying for Arabi to come and calm things down—but he must have been in the other hostage room, where the screaming had stopped, or on guard somewhere else.

"Let the boy go, at least," begged Omar, but Cheetah simply turned his back, cutting off. Fa said nothing; he was still sitting same way, with his hand shading his eyes as if he wasn't well. Seeing the terrorists so aloof, Omar crouched down beside me on his heels, and put an arm around me.

"Don't be afraid." His moustache tickled my ear, and he spoke in a hushed voice so the gunmen wouldn't get annoyed.

"It's all right, help's bound to come in time. Just say your prayers, Thomas, and try not to be afraid, they're just as scared as you are, even though right now they have the guns."

I couldn't help crying, all the same. My face was pressed against his jacket. I remember how warm and live he felt, and how the material still smelt very faintly of the aftershave lotion that he used, even after all those days in that stuffy room. It was his own special smell, and Bear liked it too. I couldn't pray then, I just sat like that, thinking, "No, no, no, no," and feeling him hug me to him, and hearing him say again, "Don't be afraid."

But I was very afraid. That the terrorists were frightened too didn't help, because no amount of pretending could alter the fact that it was they who had the guns.

There was a longish pause then, and I peered under the crook of Omar's arm to see what was happening. Miqrim was on guard. Rashid and Cheetah were over at the desk by the window. Their backs were towards us, so I couldn't see what they were doing. At last Cheetah broke away and came towards us. For the first time his gun was stuck in his waistband, and he'd left his grenade on the desk; instead of it he was holding a crystal penholder, rather like a small vase. But he'd emptied out the pens, and it now held spills of twisted paper. He went from hostage to hostage, making each take one. When he reached Mr. Mizerachi and the sick clerk he drew their spills out for them, and dropped them contemptuously by their right hands; he was enjoying himself.

We were last. He came and stood before us, straddling his legs wide, grinning. There were only two spills left, so I guessed they hadn't made one for me. Just then I hardly cared, I was staring at those two spills, almost mesmerised. Cheetah began holding them out to Fa, then thought better of it, and jerked their container back again. He took out the spills, untwisted them slowly, stared at them, then rolled them up again very deliberately before putting them back.

For once he had left his face unmuffled, and the runkled chin scar around and below his mouth lent it an evil-looking triple grin.

His thick peculiar English was slow and careful: "Number One, Number Twelve. You, English, stand up."

It seemed Fa was defying him with his usual marble-statue self-confidence. Then I saw he was trying to get up, and his legs wouldn't work. I thought, he's got cramp like I get from sitting too long in that chair. Omar had to let me go, in order to stand up and help him. He got his arm around Fa's waist, and gave him a heave—so there he was, standing as commanded before the Cheetah, but looking away from him.

Cheetah said nothing, just held out the container. Fa's right hand nudged the top, knocking it sideways. He got hold of one spill, changed his mind, and shifted to the other. The Cheetah's three grins were expanding, broad and broader, as though this tease had made his day. Fa stared at the grins with an awful intensity. At the very last second he changed his mind, grabbed at the other spill, and Cheetah stepped back, leaving it in his hand.

Fa stood there, swaying a little, not opening it. The Cheetah was still watching him while handing the last twisted spill to Omar and saying—this time in Arabic—"Yours, I think." He turned his back on us and walked away, dragging the gun from his waistband and picking up his grenade. He told Rashid, cocksure and commanding, "We'll do it now—at once. And then... after another twenty minutes—" He clicked his index finger against his gun, then pointed it at Mizerachi.

I thought neither Rashid nor Miqrim was going to argue, and I was looking and looking, from Fa to Omar and back again to Fa, and my mind went on and on repeating like a clock's hammerstrike, "Number One, Number One, Number One—" Fa had subsided on to his chair again, and I didn't even know if he'd seen what was on his piece of paper.

Omar had opened his, and was staring at it. His face didn't alter. He was pale, but he was always pale. Maybe he looked a little paler than usual, but that might have been by contrast with the blue-black prickles of his unshaved beard. He looked gravely down at me, and then back to the paper in his hand. He rolled it up again, folding it over and over on itself, quite tight, till it was only a tiny fat square in the middle of his palm.

I just sat there between them, on the floor. Omar had told me to pray, but I couldn't. Fa was my Fa after all, but Omar was specially Omar—it was going to be one of them, at once, and I couldn't pray it would be either.

16 FOR WHAT FELT like ages nobody moved, till there was the sound of running footsteps outside. Then Cheetah's grenade hand rose. But it was only Arabi who burst into the room, shouting, "No, I tell you! It's madness! Crazy—just on some stupid foreign rumour! How do you know we shan't get this plane—how do you know you won't just spoil everything when it's working out in our favour? Are we here for justice, the rights of our peoples—for our friends in prison, our cause? What is it you want—one large black headline: 'failure'?"

"Who's in command here?" yelled Cheetah.

"Not you, anyway."

Arabi closed up on Cheetah, whose left hand joggled his grenade warningly. He was crazy, you could see that—no one would play with grenades unless they were.

I could see the pulse leap in Arabi's cheek when he took hold of Cheetah's left wrist and simply pushed it aside, hanging on, not even looking at his hand to see if he would drop the grenade. He stared into Cheetah's eyes with an animal-tamer's stare. They stood like that, eyeball to eyeball, seemingly frozen.

Everyone else was absolutely frozen too. The stillness lasted a few seconds. I could see no change in Cheetah, but Arabi must have felt one: he let go of his wrist, and turned to Rashid. His voice was full and strong. "You don't go along with this, do you? Murder is murder. We all agreed—if killing can be avoided, that's right. We're so near success."

Rashid was silent, gnawing his moustache ends.

You could feel the struggle going on between the three of

them. Rashid really sick and tired of making their decisions, and wanting to hand over to someone else now the whole thing had gone on so long. Arabi trying to force leadership back into him by sheer willpower. And Cheetah's madness trying to gain control.

It seemed hours before Rashid raised his head; very slowly, but stiff and commanding. Soldierly. He said: "We will wait. And see. I shall write a note, which someone will put out through the letterbox. I will make very plain that the hostages have drawn lots, and we are not playing games." A glance at Cheetah. "If we're forced to shoot them one by one, it will not be at twenty-minute intervals. We will give them time after the first shooting, so that they fully understand us, out there. As much time as *I* think necessary, and that means as long as possible."

I'm sure Cheetah nearly rebelled. Arabi's hand hovered close to his wrist again. But Rashid had turned away, calmly, as though disobedience was impossible. He was bending over the desk, looking for more paper. He found some in the right-hand drawer. He scribbled something, paused, scribbled again. Then he read through his note, folded it, and straightened up. He stared Cheetah in the eyes as Arabi had done.

"Your grenade." He held out his hand for it.

Plainly, Cheetah couldn't believe what he was hearing. I'm sure it was the most dangerous moment of that day, but I don't think Fa had followed any bit of what was happening. It wasn't just his lack of Arabic. Slumped in the chair, he was watching Omar with an expression of horrified disbelief.

I remember praying frantically, "Not Omar—please not Omar—please not Fa."

When I looked back at the gunmen, Rashid had the grenade balanced on his palm, while the Cheetah glowered fiercely at the floor. After a moment he said, in his thick colloquial Arabic, "Give me the note, then."

"A moment." Rashid was very cool now. He put Cheetah's grenade down in the desk's 'in' tray, and opened out the note again. "We must say something else, something to twist their arm a little...yes, we'll give them the first three names to underline how serious we are. We know that Mr. Mizerachi goes second." He looked across at Fa and Omar. "Which of you gentlemen has drawn Number One?" He repeated it in his bad English. Arabi was watching, too.

There was a little pause, while I agonisingly held my breath. Then Omar said in his most matter-of-fact everyday voice, "I did." And very slowly and deliberately he opened his fingers, almost as though he was letting go of life at that moment, and the tiny bit of folded paper fluttered down on to the rug beside me. I grabbed at it, and hid it in my palm. Even then I had some crazy idea of keeping it for Bear—if I ever saw him again. But I couldn't really believe anyone would shoot Omar. It wasn't possible.

His quiet "I did" jerked the Cheetah out of his sullen withdrawal. His head rose, his mad red eyes raked the three of us. He growled out some comment that was lost in the muffling folds of his kuffieh.

"And—after the Israeli?" asked Rashid, busily writing.

It was the Lean Man. He raised a limp hand. I don't think he could speak, his voice was all locked up in his throat with terror. But the Spaniard burst out in agitation: "I—I am fourth—never, never shall I see my poor wife again! Have these devils made the women draw lots too?" No one answered him. The other hostages—except the mad clerk—were all watching Omar. They all wore the same expression, a sort of mixture of relief it wasn't them, and distress that it was him. In his quiet way he'd been our chief spokesman. Time and again he'd saved the situation, and our skins.

When I saw they did believe he could be shot—well, that made it real for me at last. I began to sob, crunching that tiny cruel slip of paper in my hand. Although Omar bent swiftly to pick me up, he didn't try to quiet me. He simply set me down by Fa in the chair, saying in a strange half-choked voice, "Here is *your* son. Comfort him."

The Cheetah tore his gaze away from us at last, and held out his hand for the note that Rashid was refolding. He strode out, heavily, and Rashid followed a moment later. Miqrim was left to guard us, and Arabi remained alone in the centre of the floor, aloof, tapping his fingers gently on his gun.

Fa put an arm around me, and patted me awkwardly on the hand. I was glad of his physical strength beside me, otherwise there was no link of special feeling, and little comfort. I just went on sobbing quietly in hiccoughs, staring at Arabi and thinking that even he could do nothing for anyone next time. We were looking at each other now, and I could see he was very sorry and upset, and I wondered if he was thinking of his little boy at home, wherever his home was.

Omar spoke directly to him, very low: "If there's more paper, I would like permission please to write a letter to my wife and son."

Arabi nodded He'd never spoken much with the adult prisoners, so his silence now didn't seem inhuman. He brought Omar the paper, and a pen from the desk—a gold one it was, heavily engraved. I suppose it was never used except for signing smart imposing letters. Omar sat down crosslegged, and thought for a moment, and then began writing rapidly in his flowing script, from right to left as Arabic is written, and digging the nib harshly now and then into the paper. I watched him in wonder. I could almost feel his pain as he wrote goodbye to Aunt Sheikhah and Alley Bear, and the way his thoughts were driving him to try to make a contact that truly couldn't be expressed in words.

Some of the other hostages begged for paper too, and began to follow his example. Fa didn't, though. Maybe he thought that I would live to be his messenger, but I thought it would be terrible if they got to Number Twelve and still he hadn't written anything for Mother. Then all I could think of was the swirl, slash, dot, flowing with such speed from Uncle Omar's pen, and that if the bus and plane weren't ready soon he would be Number One.

My sobbing had made my nose run. I wiped it on my hand, snuffling rather. Fa took his arm away to find his hanky for me, and let fall his own spill of paper. So I took it up too and put it in my pocket along with Uncle Omar's. If the gunmen ever let me go I could give that to my mother, and it would be a sort of small message if he hadn't written one, and I could lie and tell her that he'd thought of it. I was wishing very hard that I wasn't such a coward; just then I was trembling like a sick animal, and I had an animal's sixth sense that tells it when thunder is approaching, and I could sense a kind of approaching blackness in the room, an almost visible nastiness creeping from the future.

There had been too many hitches. *They* were failing us, out there: police and army, tracker dogs and guns and eyes-of-world TV cameras and none of them of any use at all.

It was about nine o'clock in the evening that Rashid came back into the room, flanked by Karim and Yusuf. His face was grim. He had a paper in his hand, and he stood in the centre of the room, the other gunmen just behind him, and read it out to us.

It was from whoever was in charge Out There. In the smoothest terms it explained regretfully that there was another hitch, unavoidable: this time the plane had developed some minor fault. Mechanics were working on it then, and just as soon as possible everything would go ahead as planned. There was something extra, too, something about international air space clearance. Somebody-in-charge begged for further patience till these troubles could be resolved.

Rashid crushed the piece of paper in his hand when he had finished reading. He dashed it to the ground as though he hated it. "A fault! Now it has a fault."

112

He said: "All right. Take him out."

They didn't have to come and fetch Omar, though. He stood up quickly, as though he had already packed himself away, life and thoughts and loves, Aunt Sheikhah and Alley Bear, and everything. He bent down and kissed the top of my head, and I felt his hand push something into my jeans pocket: the stiff, folded paper that was his note to Sheikhah and Alley Bear. He was so calm that the gunmen simply waited for him while he took off his watch and gave it to me, saying, "Wear it, and give it to Bear for me, later on. Be a brave boy, you'll come through this all right, you've done very well." Then he said to Fa, "Look after Thomas—you've got a fine son there," and he patted him on the shoulder.

Fa said nothing whatever, he was too moved to speak. I couldn't, either. Omar patted his shoulder once more, and walked away from us, looking somehow a bit smaller than usual in his correct dark suit. He didn't look back at us again—I can see him still, as he went out following Rashid: his shoulders very straight, the back of his head with its longish black hair, and the two gunmen falling in behind him, quite quietly as though they were all four going for a walk.

We heard their footsteps for a little while, then nothing.

Everyone, even the mad clerk, was quite silent. The whole building was quiet—I don't remember even traffic sounds, the sense of silent waiting was so deep.

It lasted a little while. I held Omar's watch, tightly, and looked up at Fa. He was crying.

Then there were two shots, quick, one after the other; a few seconds later came a third.

I remember thinking: they can't have. Can't, can't, can't —They have.

No one spoke for a moment, then there was an outcry of small sounds all at once, jumbled together—a prayer, a cry, a curse, a few shocked words stumbling into silence again.

Fa's face was buried in his hands, he was rocking to and fro beside me on the chair, to and fro, as I did when something made me extra miserable. I was extra miserable all right then, but there wasn't much room for me to rock too, the chair wasn't wide enough. I stared up at the ceiling, at a little round of reflected light from the rigged lamp, and wondered if Omar was like that light now he was just a body here, and if he had gone up like Elijah to heaven. And I thought without wanting to of Bear and Aunt Sheikhah waiting for him at home.

Through my grief and rage I heard Rashid's voice shouting at someone, high and edgy, "Put him outside for them to see. And tell them we'll shoot the Israeli at dawn tomorrow, unless we're on our way by then."

17 AT THAT POINT I put down my pen, and walked about the room, hating MacArthur, and brooding on the way it had all come pouring out—a three-volume novel, as Shirley said. Far too long. And too private to print. And writing it out had brought back the pain of it and I was only halfway through the worst.

I swore loudly, trudging up and down—applying all the worst words I knew in English and Arabic to MacA. My fury with him was close to that helpless rage I'd felt for those terrorists when they took Omar away. Suddenly I could stand that room no longer, and I flung out of it, leaving the papers strewn about the desk, and went off home, thinking, I'll leave it—tear it up. Just won't finish it. MacArthur couldn't make me after all...

But that night and the next morning Day Four of the siege went on and on forcing itself into my reluctant thoughts: black, inescapable. It had to be exorcised somehow. At teatime I grabbed myself a mug and stale bun, and headed back to the purgatorial task again.

The first thing I noticed was that someone had tidied the strewn papers into a neat pile and their correct order. Mac-Arthur, or Shirley? Or somebody else? Anyway, a zealous hand had made things ready for me. Oh, come on, Zed, I told myself, don't shirk it now... I sat down and took up my pen again, pushing the chocolate aside; it wasn't needed.

It was like the end of the world, that moment when Omar was led away. The space on my right, where he'd always sat or lain, was something I couldn't look at. I had leant on him so,

115

and now there was just that space. And since those shots the terrorists weren't people. They were something inhuman, to speak to them would be like trying to talk with tigers. Of course, Cheetah had always been that way.

I remember that the palms of my hands were soaking wet Secretly I dried them on Fa's sleeve, but they were wet again at once. I leaned heavily against him, and was rocked to and fro by his rocking, yet I somehow knew that he barely noticed me. At least we were grieving for Omar together, which was a warmth, a kind of bond. And at least Fa had drawn the end number—I tried to comfort myself by thinking that we were bound to be rescued before they got to Number Twelve, anyway; *if* Rashid remained in charge and was making the decisions.

It must be quite dark outside now. What would it be like out there? First, the shots would have worried them, and then...they had seen Omar... My thoughts shied away from that. Perhaps more police, or army, had been hurried in. Fire engines too, maybe, and searchlights.

Somewhere in cosy little boxes of brightly-lit rooms boys and girls my age and younger would be watching it all on television with their parents. "And now over to So-and-so at Regency Gate—blah-blah—"

Just an evening show for them. Before cocoa and biscuits and bedtime.

And Omar was dead. I wondered if Aunt Sheikhah knew yet. Alley Bear would be asking again and again when his Baba was coming home. (Baba is Arabic for father.) Four days. He must have cried a lot. As I was crying now, only more noisily.

By and by I began to cry less, and needed to go to the lavatory. I couldn't bear to ask the gunmen, so I held on till my need was so urgent that I had to ask. Yahia was guarding us. He was jumpier still since the shooting, and at first paid me no attention. Then he went to the door and shouted for

Yusuf or Arabi.

It was Arabi who came. I wouldn't look at him. I just said sullenly, "I want to go." He walked behind me down the passage, and I walked as fast as I could to get away from him. Usually they made us keep the door open, but I shut it, and he didn't object. When I'd done, I didn't pull. I wanted to stay in there away from everyone, as hidden as a rabbit in its hole. I stood for some while in the farthest corner, my forehead against the wall. I felt empty, even of fear. My eyes hurt with so much crying, and tears kept on rolling out, making them hotter still.

Suddenly I got in a state of panic, in case I'd let Omar's letter fall down the pan, when I unzipped myself. It could so easily have happened! I grabbed at my back pocket, and hastily turned it inside out. The note fell on to the floor, and with it the two spills.

I heaved an enormous sigh, wobbly with relief, and buttoned the note very carefully away, inside my shirt pocket this time. Then I picked up the spills. Maybe I should give Fa's back to him, the terrorists might ask for it? But I'd keep Omar's for myself, if we got out of here. Aunt Sheikhah would have the letter, and Bear the watch, and I would have the spill, the little square which had been almost the last thing Omar handled . . . just to hold it then made me feel steadier; though maybe I ought to give it to Bear when he was big enough to understand, and tell him how calm Uncle Omar had been as he folded it over and over again, and answered Rashid's question in a steady voice. I wondered how he felt when he opened it, and found Number One . . . he'd shown no fear at all.

I scarcely realised that I'd smoothed it out while I was thinking; and then suddenly it was there open in my hand, though all creased in little squares. In the centre was scrawled '12'.

My first thought was that I must have mixed them up—

and this was Fa's. But he'd rolled his up again, just like it was at first. I unrolled it, hardly daring to, and looked at it. And then back at Omar's.

I was still staring at them when Arabi's voice said, low and worried: "Thomas Zed! Are you all right in there?"

I tore Fa's spill into shreds and threw them down the pan. The little white fragments went round and round in the rush of water, then disappeared. I opened the door and came out.

Now I was really face to face with Arabi for the first time since it happened. He looked different, somehow: paler and more stern, and something deeper. (I guess now it was hopelessness.) His dark eyes, very intent, searched my face. He said, simply: "I'm sorry, Thomas Zed."

I would have said, "You killed him," but I couldn't, not now. I didn't speak, I just walked back to the room ahead of him. He put his hand on my shoulder, and I shook it off.

Outside the room I stopped, not wanting to go in. But I'd no choice. Arabi gave me a firm but gentle push before he turned away. Holding Omar's paper, hardly aware of what I did, I crossed to Fa and put it in his hand. He looked down on it, not knowing what it was. And then knowing. And I saw that he knew *I* knew, and was crying in the same way I had, although not for the same reason. I was feeling all sorts of things at the same time—hatred and misery, and very, very sorry for him. I couldn't bear to see him like that. For the second time my world had cracked apart and there was nothing underneath.

Hesitantly I put my hand on his knee. He shoved me away hard and angrily, saying, "It was only for *you*."

Wood scraped my knees as I went sprawling on the floor, the paper fell beside me.

Up till then I'd always managed to hang on, somehow. Even at the worst moment of Omar's death. Somehow, somewhere, a distant though benevolent God who had different names in my prayers and Alley Bear's would put out a kindly hand and make everything all right again, impossible though it might seem. I'd been waiting for a miracle. Even Omar's death itself I'd falsified into a round of light up on the ceiling, somehow connected to the old, old stories of Elijah going up to heaven.

Now I just lay on my face and gave up. I didn't mind what happened any more, so long as it was quick; yet at one level I was more afraid than ever, because I had no one left. There must really have been a strong link between me and Fa, an odd link perhaps, but a looking-up-to and down-on uneven sort of bond. Omar had known it, even if it wasn't a warm and happy one like his and Bear's. That was why—

Omar had done it for me, and Fa had accepted it, and I was lumbered with that for ever. But Fa hadn't done it for me, that hating push away from him had told me that. We were both cowards, horrible cowards, horribly afraid to die, horribly unfit to live. If I got out of here alive I would never be fit for anything again.

I remember a shocked silence in the room, but not one of the other hostages said or did anything. I put my arms closely over my head, hugging it, and curled myself into a ball, and lay with my eyes screwed up tight. After a while I began to shake more and more, till my feet were almost drumming on the floor. There was blackness in my mind, sickness in my stomach, a world outside me as frightful as a tiger's spring.

Time stretched out endlessly, no one touched me, there was no sound but footsteps coming in and out of the room, and once a low-voiced argument by the door between two gunmen. The words reached me, but strung together into nothing. They were senseless sounds—maybe it was because the world itself had lost all sense for me. I do remember that I tried to understand and couldn't. It was like being a very small baby again: I just heard speech as noise. Perhaps I'd never, ever understand what people said to me again. Perhaps I wouldn't want to.

18 LOCKED AWAY AS I was inside myself, I only gradually grew aware of someone bending over me, to pick me up. I thought it was Fa and went rigid, eyes still tight shut.

"You come and sit with me, Thomas Zed," said Arabi.

The words were just quick sounds one after the other: pitter and pitter, pat-a-pat. And I was small, very small, a baby.

"Fa, Omar, gun shoot . . . Fa." My eyes still tight shut.

"No, no shooting now. Over here."

Arabi held me beneath the arms, swung me across the room, and lowered me on to a rug.

Immediately I curled up tight again, still shaking, and put my thumb in my mouth and sucked it. "Da," I said. "Da-da-da-da." It makes me want to puke now, when I remember it. Still, that's how it was. It was partly real, and partly me acting to myself. Arabi sat down beside me on the rug. He put his hand on my wrist, and pulled my thumb gently from my mouth. "No, you're not a baby, stop that, Thomas Zed. *Stop it.*"

That got through to me all right; it jerked me alive to everything and to myself—as mad as fire, both with him and me. My shaking stopped, perhaps it turned into all that anger: fuelled it, somehow.

"You shot him."

Arabi sighed, deeply, hopelessly. He just shook his head.

"You *did*—because you all did—even my F—" I stopped, hurriedly. It was a great crushing weight on my tongue, it crushed all of us: the other hostages, Fa alone in the big chair,

Yahia already guarding us for the night, standing near the door with a gun ready in his hand. Yahia looked ready to drop—that was Omar's death too, weighing him down. I looked up into Arabi's face.

"Even—?" He looked across at Fa, frowning.

"No," I said fiercely, "no. It wasn't, he didn't, it was you—only all of you."

Arabi said nothing, he was still staring at Fa, eyes narrowed. I didn't want him to know, now—I would have taken my words back if I could. But his mind was as lightning-sharp as his gunman's reactions. He held something out to me: that revealing piece of paper, creased in tiny squares. He must have picked it off the floor when he picked me up.

"This . . . was it your Uncle's? Number Twelve?"

"It was my Fa's—it was." But I heard the lie in my voice.

Arabi was silent.

I said fiercely, "I hate you. I hate you all."

When he did speak, Arabi said, "It's good you can still get angry. There's good stuff there, Thomas Zed."

I didn't understand what he meant. We were stuck in a black hole of guns and fear and hate, and I could see nothing good in it at all.

My anger was draining away, my thumb went to my mouth again. Fragile as glass I was, the only thing holding me together was that thumb. This time Arabi didn't stop me. I wanted to stand up and walk away from him, but my legs were boneless, no joints, no shape. I thought how ashamed of me my mother would be. I stared up at the rigged light, and wished someone would switch it off for good. Against it I kept seeing Omar's head, very erect as he walked away towards blackness, towards—

Perhaps the light was good. Better than—

I sucked my thumb, sucked and sucked it. Better. Better like Bear on Aunt Sheikhah's lap, safe, never standing up again . . . But I was behind Omar's eyes, looking out at two

121

gunmen, seeing the shiny barrels rising, blackness in their mouths that were hungry for redness, never Elijah's golden chariot, just—Then it was my Fa's face hovering, staring heavy hatred, saying, "It was for *you*." Pushing me away.

Shut eyes tight, suck thumb, cut off. But still see Omar going out the room—Over and over again, Omar going out the room—

I can't guess how long it was before I knew someone had dimmed the lamp. It must have been late. Arabi was lying by me on the rug, cat-napping, breathing gently, in, out, as Omar would never breathe again. His face was all hollows, the pulse in his cheek barely flickered. I could see every bluish prickle of his beard; his moustache wasn't silky like Omar's, but rough, ragged by this time, and pirate-looking, almost hiding the lines of his mouth, which were wide, firm and curved. Perhaps he felt my staring, for he opened his eyes. They were anxious and sad. Omar's enemy, who killed him.

"Thomas Zed, you're very young to have had all this happen to you."

"I hate you, you shot him. All of you." My voice sounded weak, stupid, my eyes were hot and irritable. I rubbed them, hard.

He didn't protest. He just gave a long-drawn sigh. He spoke very softly, so that Yahia couldn't hear. "It has finished us. We've failed—I think we'll all be dead by morning. You shall go safe, though. Believe me, I know it deep inside myself."

I believed him—for I too knew things in that way. I'd known Omar would die. Now I knew I'd never feel safe again. Anywhere.

"But when he died you lost your father. I wish I could give him back to you."

Confused by that, I thought he meant Omar. Then I knew he didn't.

I didn't answer.

He sighed again, murmuring, "It *was* a good cause... I think we were right to try. The world won't understand, though. *She* didn't understand—"

I saw tears come into his brown eyes, and knew he wasn't speaking to me then. He put his hand inside his shirt pocket, and drew out some small square snapshots, plain cheap black and white prints. He nursed them in his palm. I heard him murmur, "I should have destroyed these—mustn't be traced back to them—" Squinting sideways, I saw by the faint light that one snap was of a woman, young and smiling, with a straight proud neck. She had one arm around a little boy. He was laughing, and his face was rather blurred, but there was something about the way he stood, foursquare, his stomach thrust out, that was so like Bear. The other snap was quite clear. It was of Arabi himself, with his cheek pressed against a small child's. Arabi looked younger, his moustache was clipped into a thin line, and the child was the boy of the other photograph, I thought.

"He too will be fatherless by morning," Arabi was saying. "My Feisal—who will comfort him—who will care for his future? They'll say we were dogs, and the sons of dogs."

I didn't want to be sorry. I said, "But it's your fault."

"Perhaps, but—the world's fault too, Thomas Zed. It's too many things that happen—" he made a vague gesture—"out there." He was looking at those photographs still. He bent and kissed them fiercely, regardless of my stare. I think he meant to tear them up then, but couldn't bring himself to do it yet. He put them back into their hiding-place again.

I didn't quite understand what he had said—but maybe it was true somehow, since no one seemed to be in control any more, least of all Fa; and after all it wasn't Arabi who shot Omar, he'd been the one who always stood out for waiting. I fell against him suddenly in a passion of weeping. "It's Bear, it's Bear—why did you all do it to them, why? Why to us?

123

Why Uncle Omar? Why to *him*?" I meant Arabi's son.

I was clutching at him with both hands, warm and sticky. He put his arms around me—the first time he'd let go of his gun. For a moment I thought that he was Omar in a way, and I was both Bear and Arabi's son, the little boy whose name was Feisal, whose other name I didn't know.

Arabi was saying in my ear, "He was a brave man. Don't cry for him—you live for him, see, that's much harder—it will be a very brave thing to do. You'll live to go home, and tell *his* son how he died, Thomas Zed—"

"How could I?" I choked against his chest. "I haven't got a home—now. It was because of me . . . I can't—not holding Fa's hand . . . and my legs won't work, they've gone funny—I wasn't much good, ever."

"Now see." His firm hands took hold of my shoulders, and held me a bit away from him. "This is untrue. You've survived as well as anyone here, haven't you? And you only eight."

"I cried . . . I shook."

"So did most of them—when they thought no one would see. And they grown men." He gave a very faint smile. "And I—I am nearly crying now. It's been a terrible time, Thomas Zed. Perhaps you'll never have to endure such a time again, in your whole life. But it's not over yet, you must be brave a little longer, it won't last for ever. After this, you can truly say you know the worst and the best—of other people—and yourself. We're all really very much alike—"

I thought of Fa and Omar.

As though he knew what I was thinking, he said, "Try not to take everything too hard—there are moments when some of us are a little weaker, or braver—a little crueller—or kinder—Just that small difference maybe you—we—can choose, but—" He said a lot more, urgently, as though he was speaking to his Feisal as well as to me: things about sons and fathers that I closed my mind to then, though I remembered them later, word for word.

I looked at him, and he was finishing a sentence: "—but never be too quick to blame other people, try to understand."

His hands pushed me away a bit more, then left my shoulders. "Now you are you, only. You don't need to hold anyone's hand, after tonight, Thomas Zed. Because you can manage anything. It's a sort of coming of age. So let's have a new name for you, not Thomas. Let's call you—Zed. That's a good short, strong name, eh? And it suits you, short as you are."

My legs were still shaking, shamefully. They rattled on the floor like dice. It was Omar and the gun.

Again Arabi understood. He picked up his gun, and held it so that I was looking straight down the muzzle. "Look. That's all he saw—A little round black moment, and then—That's all it is: moments. Moment of birth, moment you first go to school, moment someone is unfair or cruel to you, moment you make love, moment you die. Try to understand, Zed. Nothing in this world lasts very long, so why shake about it? He didn't, and you won't, Zed."

I stared down the gun's mouth, into its small black eye, and it was all true, what he said, every word. I just felt a great sadness about Omar, and some fear of what might happen still, but my legs stopped shaking.

"Ah," said Arabi, after a moment, "that's better. Now you come over here, and we'll share some chocolate, and then you sleep. That would be good, eh?" From his other pocket he pulled a bar of that very black bitter chocolate which has a rich dry taste. Strangely enough, I felt hungry for it. I didn't think Uncle Omar would have minded my sharing with Arabi. In fact, I thought he might be glad.

I'd only hesitated the fraction of a second, but Arabi said: "Your uncle wouldn't mind. We held very different views, but there was no enmity between us—he was a very generous man." He broke off some squares of bitter chocolate, and gave them to me. I ate some straight away, but I was suddenly too tired to finish them. My head spun. I just remember curling up on the rug, some chocolate still in my hand, my head hard against Arabi's thin muscular chest. He held me like that, his gun resting cold across my shoulder.

"So. Sleep now, Zed."

Once in the night I woke. Yusuf guarded the door. Fa was still slumped in the chair. The other hostages were quiet or snoring. Arabi lay quiet too, his eyes closed. I thought he was maybe catnapping, but his gun-arm holding me was tense. The light cast whiteness and shadow on his face, and there were deep marks beneath his eyes like runnels, almost as though he had been crying. His free hand rested on his shirt pocket where the snapshots were. I went to sleep again.

19 I WAS WOKEN by a crash so loud that I thought the outer wall must have collapsed. Arabi leapt up, rolling me clear with his foot, and yelling, "'Keep down." He swivelled towards the window, which seemed to be coming in on us, shutters and all—feet swinging in between them, feet of hurtling black shapes, space age and faceless. A second stunning explosion didn't hurt, except my ears. A barrage of sound, an underlying ominous rattle. For seconds I held an impression of Arabi straddling the air, groping hands flung high, clawing, climbing upwards, then he crashed back on to the floor and his gun fell painfully on top of me, and it was someone else this time yelling, "*Down*—keep down!"

"How many? Two?"

"Both."

Not understanding, I began crawling towards Arabi, thinking: he's hurt, he must be—

Someone grabbed me bodily from behind, and flung me towards a blackness by the door. I was caught and hurled on again, swooping clean along the corridor into another pair of hands. Light flared in the hall below, women were screaming somewhere, figures grappling, a trail of fire on the stairs. I was scooped up again and carried through another room and down a fire escape. Other people hustled by, heels struck iron. In the hushed darkness of the garden, beneath a cool dawn sky, there was a pool of concentrated light: a squat searchlight, throwing a fierce beam on to the fire escape. Black figures, uniformed figures, crossed its barrier, ascending or descending.

I shut my eyes while I was carried through the glare, and

opened them to see pale faces peering up at us. Such noise behind us, shouts, shooting, a barrage of bangs.

"Can you walk now, kid?"

"Yes," I whispered, and was put down on to grass.

"Over there, see?"

I stumbled forward, helped by a guiding hand towards a knot of people. A policewoman tried to hold me. I butted her with my head, slipped beneath her arm, and scuttled between another group of shadowy forms into the shelter of some lilac bushes. My chest was heaving—breath wasn't going in and out quite right, everything wavered around me, disappearing mistily, reappearing, then misty again. I clung to a low-hanging branch, and fought for breath. The clean fresh smell of dewy leaves and pungent earth revived me. I stayed very still, like an animal, leaning against my branch.

A woman's shrill voice was crying, "That child . . . he's run off! Find him—"

I peered from my hiding-place. Safe enough, because I was in darkness beyond the pool of light thrown by the toad-squat searchlight. Inside the building there were still shouts and shooting, some little dancing flames at a high window. Now and then figures surged through the searchlight beam, going up or down. Some came down grotesquely humpbacked with heavy bundles. I couldn't tell what was happening, or who was in or out. I thought of Fa in his chair. Arabi on the floor.

I went in a wide semi-circle through the bushes, keeping to shadows. I waited till no one was on the fire escape, then crept up the first few treads in darkness, and crossed the bright path just below the windows at a run.

There were cries of: "What's that child doing?" "Come back here, kid!" from beneath. Footsteps pounded across grass, gravel, and the first iron rungs.

I climbed in through the open window, keeping low, scraping my knees on the sill. There was still firing somewhere, but not near, and a smoky smell. I walked upright, feeling oddly immune: a ghost-child—bullets would go straight through me and do no harm. A bunch of people were coming towards me, shepherded by a man in black. I thrust my way between them, like someone going the wrong way on an escalator. Fa was there, moving slowly in the direction of the fire escape. He had one arm over the African's broad shoulder and, head hanging, was being helped along. I said, "Fa—?" But he didn't seem to hear or see me. I was invisible. I still had this strange feeling that everyone was powerless to stop me, even the men in black. Maybe it was my smallness: in this gloomy wrecked place they hardly noticed me, or maybe there was still too much activity in the hall below. Only the Spaniard muttered, "Maria!" as I bumped against his legs. I passed him, and still nobody stopped me.

I reached the threshold of our old room, where we'd been imprisoned. The wrecked shutters swung wide, and cold air and smokiness had almost conquered smell and fug. It was strange to be there without a terrorist on guard, and I began to shiver, though not from fear, more from the oddness of everything. "Just moments", Arabi had said.

I stood in the middle of the room, looking about me. The rigged light leaned crazily sideways, pointing its beam downward, lighting the pinks and reds of the thick Persian rug where I'd been sleeping—the colour spilt right across the floor. Arabi wasn't there.

Voices behind me said: "What in God's name?"

"Shocked . . . must be, doesn't he know his father's out?"

"You come along—Thomas, isn't it?"

I was lifted, slung over a shoulder. A burly arm held me there. "Zed," I said, into somebody's dark blue collar, silver-numbered.

This time I was carried fast, not thrown. There were drifts of blue smoke, no flames, and a hissing spray of water, as we retraced our steps towards the fire escape.

"Look, your father's down there now, OK?" said the

young policeman as we descended. "Not hurt, are you?"

I shook my head, saying, "No" and "I can walk."

We reached the gravel and he put me down, keeping a hand on my shoulder, steering me towards a group of people. "Don't you try going up there again, now your Dad's out! We've had enough trouble, I can tell you. Look, there he is—"

"Arabi. Where is he?"

He didn't understand. "Yes, I told you—your Dad's over there" He gave me a gentle shove towards Fa, who was standing a little apart, all alone now, hunch-shouldered, staring at the ground. I drifted in his direction, between other people. Most stood silent, maybe unable to believe that they were free. The Spaniard was hugging his wife, then both went down on their knees together: giving thanks, I suppose.

I skirted them, looked back and saw the policeman turn away. Fa still stood alone, but I went past him, unnoticed and searching, though I knew in my heart that Arabi couldn't be out here among us all, free.

There was a sudden exultant shout. I looked up where everyone was looking, and saw two of the terrorists being brought down the escape, handcuffed together. They looked so small and shabby and ordinary now they were beaten— once-powerful Rashid and scarred Karim. When they reached the ground a wave of dark blue and silver surrounded them, and they were quick-marched away, small and scared and hopeless by the growing light of a pinkish dawn, already dappled with grey cloud.

One or two of the hostages jeered, but most stood in silence, watching. While everyone's attention was elsewhere I edged away again, out of sight of watchful eyes, and skirting the lilac bushes. I must find out what they'd done with Arabi—he was nowhere here. He must have been wounded. Perhaps they'd taken him out through the front entrance?

Then I saw: literally almost stumbled on them—dark

bundles on the grass verge, flung down casually under the flowering almond.

He was the nearest. He was lying with his face slightly turned towards the light, and his limbs sprawled out as though he was asleep, though his eyes were open, staring up into the flowery branches that were moving gently in the chilly air. At first I thought he was scattered with some fallen petals . . . only it was too bright a red.

I crept nearer, forcing myself on somehow. Closer, closer —till I could see the shining in his eyes that was only reflection. I knelt down beside him, and the grass was icy wet to my knees, though when I touched his hand it was still warm. There was something I had to do, and quickly, before I had time to be too much afraid.

There was no red on his shirt pocket. I was thankful for that, at least—if there had been I couldn't have touched him. I put my hand in quickly, groping for the little squares of card. They were still there, no one had searched him yet. Their edges pricked my fingers as I drew them out face upwards—the pictures of his wife and Feisal who was so near Bear's age, and Arabi himself who had comforted me last night—and I pushed them deep into my own shirt pocket, with Omar's note.

Then there was nothing more—just a funny dreamlike sense of birdsong and shouting and London waking-up noises all going round and round above me in the almond tree, as if the wind-whipped branches were turning a disc on the record player by my bed at home, with Arabi's face, no light in his eyes, at the disc's centre that was growing darker and blacker as it played.

20 MUCH LATER, THEY told me I had fainted. ("Poor kid—do you wonder?") It was a very long faint. The next thing I remember is a booming sound above the top of my head, some way off, something I didn't want to hear. It was combined with a touch on my shoulder which made it ache. I was one large ache, and I wrapped myself tighter, deeper, into my eiderdown, and made it part of my body; no use, the boom grew louder, the touch heavier, bass sound turned into words:

"Nothing but exhaustion... seems to have come through very well. Let him sleep."

My mother's voice, with an unfamiliar worried note to it, answered, "That *is* all? You're quite sure?"

"Certainly, yes..." boom, boom "...eye on him. Clean him up a bit when he wakes." Boom. "...come back later in the day."

A heavy tread crossed the floor. Our doctor's a very big man. A long way off the telephone was shrilling, cut off when Christl answered it.

I was back in my own room, all right.

"Call in at the hospital too. See your husband."

"You've been so very kind—"

Boom "...nothing." The door clicked to.

Hah, I thought, working the eiderdown into a close cocoon, a green cave, my haven. Let them be kind, I didn't want them, so long as that eiderdown was packed safely round me, green—not red—

Red. Panic—had they undressed me? I felt. No—only my socks. And no wonder our Doctor said "clean him up", I was

132

still in the same clothes that had gone all through the siege. And with that thought came others, everything hit me at once, till the cocoon was useless and I sat up wanting to scream, just holding it back, as my fingers scrabbled, sweaty and shaking, at my pocket. Suppose Mother came back into the room and found me awake, she'd tell Christl to start on the cleaning. Had anyone looked in my pocket yet? It was all right, the snaps were there with the note, no one had found and taken them, it was all right—

There was an unfamiliar easy chair by my bed. Someone must have been sitting with me—Mother?

The note was Aunt Sheikhah's. I put it on the chair. But Arabi had meant to destroy his photographs. I sat holding them, not wanting to look at them, not wanting to see again the red not-flowers on Arabi's shirt. Then I remembered him holding out his gun, telling me to look down the barrel, saying that everything was just for a moment, not to take it all too hard.

So I looked at them, and knew I could never tear them up, though no one else should see them, or the small brownish stain across the back of one. They were my secret. A special talisman of courage. Something, like Omar's piece of paper, that was Arabi's. And they should go into my usual hiding-place.

My eiderdown was a comforting nest, but I got out of it, shuddering as my feet met cold floor, and padded across to my cupboard which I kept locked against the ravages of Alley Bear. The key was just above it on a shelf out of his reach. I unlocked the door, and groped for my miniature train set which fitted into a plastic mould. No one would find the photographs, hidden in the hollows beneath the mould. I slid them in, relocked the cupboard, and made a flying leap back into bed.

My bed. Amazing. Somewhere I never expected to be again. But inside me the ache of misery was beginning, worse than the worst toothache: for Omar, for Arabi, for a dark head going out of the door, for red flowers under the almond tree, for Bear—My green eiderdown cave welcomed me, a refuge before the struggle with moments would begin.

I woke for the second time, and the telephone was ringing again. On and on. After a while it stopped, and a few minutes later the doorbell rang. There were voices in the passage, Christl's voice shouting at someone, then the front door was slammed, and I heard my mother's voice upraised: "Why can't they leave us alone? You'd think they'd realise..." I wondered who "they" were. The phone rang again. "Christl!" she yelled. "Leave the receiver off."

Next, something happened that I'd dreaded—Aunt Sheikhah's quick, light footsteps approached my door. I wanted to pretend that I was sleeping—once, I would have done. I pulled myself up in the eiderdown, and sat gripping my knees. She pushed the door open very gently, saw me sitting there awake, and came in. Her poor face was all swollen and blotched with crying, but she managed to smile at me.

"Thomas."

It sounded strange, now I was Zed.

She sat down on my bed, and put her arms around me, her soft cheek against mine. "*You* came back anyway. They tell me you were so very brave."

I shook my head. My face was muffled against her. "He was."

I pulled myself away, to grope for the folded paper on the chair. I couldn't look at her.

"He gave it to me—it's for you." I thrust it into her hand, and stared at my wrists. Then I realised something was missing. "His watch was for Bear! Someone's taken it."

"It's all right, they took it off and gave it to me." It was a whisper, I could hardly hear her. There was a long pause. I thought she was reading Uncle Omar's letter, but when I looked up she was just sitting gazing at it in her hand. She made an odd sound, suddenly, and got up and walked out of the room, stumbling against the door as though she didn't see it.

The next footsteps were my mother's. She came into the room forcefully, a great fat wind blowing, her blue dress billowing out about her fatness, the heavy scent she wore quite drowning the smell of me. She had a floating gauzy scarf around her neck, and a half-knitted baby garment trailed from huge wooden needles in her hand. It was Christl's knitting on Christl's needles. She looked at the empty chair by my bed, and the creepy awareness that I sometimes possessed made me know she was thinking, "I should have been sitting with him."

She dumped herself down on it now, and began knitting very fast saying, "You'll need a bath, Thomas, when you get up. Pfui!" She wrinkled her nose. "You'll need clean bed-clothes, too."

I nodded. This sort of thing made me feel at home. At least, it didn't matter any more. If she'd been there, in that house, she'd have been in with the other women, in her billowing blue dress.

"I'm all right to get up now."

"Are you sure?" She stopped knitting, and looked relieved. "There's some soup on the way, aren't you hungry? Wouldn't you like something to eat first?"

She was really trying quite hard. It was such an effort for us both that it made me feel weak again. I shook my head. "I'm not hungry." I said, rather surprised that I wasn't. I was pleating the green stuff of my eiderdown between my fingers, and she said rather irritably, "Oh, don't do that—" pulling herself up halfway through the scold. But I hadn't minded, that way she seemed just as usual, and it was more comfortable. I stopped pleating, and said, "Mother . . . why's Father in hospital? He wasn't—He didn't *look* hurt."

She frowned, dropped a stitch, and picked it up the wrong way round.

"No, he wasn't hurt, but—Oh, I don't know, blood pressure—some check on his heart—Why do you always ask questions? Well, never mind," she said handsomely, "you can't help it, I suppose you had a rough time too. We did, I can tell you. And poor Yola's taking it badly—such a mistake to marry a Saudi, I was always telling her. And a Muslim too, I don't know what they do about funerals, some rite I suppose. Did you remember to say your prayers?"

"Quite a lot, really."

"Good boy. But of course she's got Bear—though that will be difficult if his family cast her off, and I bet they'll seize the first chance, they never accepted her, the old man's other sons will be down on the perks like ravens. That sort of Arab or Turk—how they go on about honour and obligations! Well, now we shall see. Your father's being most annoying, swears he won't go out there on holiday now."

"You've dropped another stitch."

"So I have. Never mind, Christl's knitting is a bird's nest, anyway. What was I saying? Of course we'll do what we can but that won't be much—all these disgraceful taxes, petrol, our entertaining—and your school—"

"But I thought we were quite rich?"

"Peanuts, darling, by today's standards. What do you know about it? I daresay my own family would help if she'd make up her mind to be sensible, get her child baptized, and come back to the Faith—she's stubborn, though, a bit of a fool. Always took the wrong course and always will, I suppose. Well, thank God there are State schools here, and Bear seems a bright enough child, he'll probably settle down very well."

"It's run."

"What has?"

"The stitch."

"You might have told me. Christl's taking her time over that soup. If they'd only kept you in hospital—but Yola thought you'd be happier home, I daresay she was right. Your father—*did* he have pain in the chest?"

"He didn't say so." (Perhaps he had pain. Perhaps he felt so ill he didn't know what he was doing. Oh God, let me at least believe it was like that.)

"They did keep some people in...debriefing, they said. And perhaps...because of your uncle—" She shot me a quick look. "We can go and visit tomorrow. you can take him some flowers, you'd like that, wouldn't you?"

Red flowers. From Uncle Omar.

"What was all that telephoning?" I asked, so as not to answer.

"Oh, people...Press. You'll have to do some talking, Thomas, you know that, don't you? Not the Press, to the police. The doctor thinks maybe tomorrow."

An awful lot seemed to be happening tomorrow.

"You needn't worry, they'll be nice to you. A very good-looking sympathetic young man came to ask about you. *He* saw just what I'd been through. Quite a good suit too, public money, I suppose. He'll simply ask you some questions."

Click, click, went her needles. Christl would have a lovely mess to straighten out.

"Questions?" But I knew: which gunmen shot...that dark head going out the door...

Suddenly I said, "I want to see Bear! I want to see him now, before I get up! *I want!*" I felt small and weak and Thomas again. My fingernails dug hard through the eider-down into my knees.

She jumped up, dropping the baby garment. Blueness bellied over me, a huge sail, the big curls of her black hair bounced on the frill above her breasts.

"Now don't start upsetting yourself. You'll upset him

137

again, he keeps asking and asking for Omar, it's driving everyone mad."

"I won't upset him, I won't, I promise—if I could just see Bear?" A huge effort stopped my voice from wobbling. *Zed.* "Couldn't I have some soup now, and then can't I see him? *Then* I could get up and have my bath."

That seemed to decide and reassure her. She sailed from the room calling in the warm, crooning tone she sometimes used, "Christl! My poor child's hungry, hurry up and bring that soup, don't be all night about it."

Bear came at last, his fat pink cheeks were pale. Stupidly, I'd forgotten to ask how much he knew. He was carrying Mustafa, velvet orange carrot and all. In the daytime he generally had his drum. He climbed up on my bed, pushing the donkey ahead of him, and thrust his round head and bulging cheeks against my chest. I pulled the green eider-down over the three of us, till we were in a warm breathy cave, light just shining a little bit through.

"Hullo, Bear, Hullo, Mustafa." I switched to Arabic— Bear had quite a few English words, French too, but he didn't use them much.

"Gone away." he said sadly. "Not coming long time— when? When, Thomas?"

I didn't say anything. The donkey's heavily-sucked ear was beneath my chin.

"When?"

"I don't know, chum." I rocked him a little. "Your donkey's been swimming."

"Didn't say goodbye."

"Yes, he did. Don't you remember? You were eating breakfast and he picked you up and kissed you... you had food all over your face and it came off on his moustache." I gulped. Mustafa's right ear was handy, and I chewed it hard. "Moustache—pet dog..." Bear laughed suddenly. "When's he coming back, Thomas?"

"Look," I said, desperate, "I've got another name now, just between you and me. It's Zed."

"Zed, that's a funny—You smell, Zed. When's—"

"I'm going to have a bath, soon. Where's your derbakki drum?"

"I beat 'n beat it, then it went right through, then it went away. Mummy's been crying."

I was afraid he was going to start again, and I said quickly, "Well, you'll have to get another. Or—I tell you what, we'll get you a mouth organ. That's more fun, that's different."

"How will we?"

There was quite a lot of money in my moneybox, tips and things. "Well, the fact is, *he* gave me some money, for you. It was a secret. He said, 'I'm going away, maybe for some while, maybe a very long time, it's sudden, so you must take this and buy Bear a surprise present from me, an extra special present.' So you and I and Mustafa and Christl will go and buy it."

He thought for a minute. I held my breath. My powers of invention were running out.

"He did say goodbye?"

"Yes, I told you. And the present's an extra special goodbye, isn't it?"

"When will we get it, Zed? When?"

"When I've had my bath, chum. If they'll let us. Up we get."

21 THE MOUTH ORGAN seemed to comfort Bear, a little. We got it just before the shop closed for the night, he and I and Christl creeping out by the back entrance of the flats, because of reporters waiting round the front with flashlights. Even so, one determined woman caught up with us. "No comment," hissed Christl, hustling me ahead, and shielding Bear beneath her arm. I was on the front page next day, thin-faced and stick-armed. "Siege victim's son goes shopping," ran the headline. They said how tall I was for four years old.

Alley Bear played the mouth organ a great deal, piercingly, with a strong penetrating sense of rhythm. Aunt Sheikhah didn't seem to notice, she was walking round in a kind of daze, not paying attention to anyone or anything; answering at random if you spoke to her, and that was all. She cuddled Bear when he cried, but mostly he played the mouth organ, somehow making it sound like an Arabian wail of mourning for Uncle Omar.

My mother was cross. "Very thoughtless of you, Thomas! And if you're well enough to think of things like mouth organs, you could have talked more to the police—that pleasant boy came again, he seems to think I'm amazingly calm after my ordeal. I told him he didn' understand the strength of Lebanese women. He's coming back tomorrow." Then she was quiet and specially kind for a bit, in a peculiar sort of way.

We were back to normal next day, with an argument before starting for the hospital. A car was coming for us at about eleven, and I'd said I didn't want to go.

"He'll be extremely hurt—his only son! Not well enough to visit him, but well enough for mouth organs—what will people think?"

"I'm well. I just don't want to, and I don't care what people think."

"He's a hero, so they say in all the papers. You should be very proud of him. You'll come with me and like it. Start behaving like a hero's son, for a change. Go and find some clean socks, and brush your hair—heavens, don't wipe your nose on your hand, get a handkerchief! You can wait for me on the hall chair, and don't stir until I'm ready."

I was sitting there biting my nails when Christl came by with some ironing.

"Was there something in the papers about Fa?" I asked. My mother had kept them from me—on the doctor's advice, she said. I saw no need to tell Christl that.

"You did not know?" She put down the clothes, and ran to find the paper. A kind girl, Christl. She showed me Fa's picture—in hospital, pretty nurse holding his pulse—and then read a bit out to me (she liked to improve her English accent). "'Mr. Amstrill'—they got the name wrong, Thomas—'was admired for his coolness throughout the four-day ordeal. "A dialogue with the terrorists was essential," Mr. Amstrill told me from his hospital bed. "We all did our best to keep on easy terms with them. Knowing the Middle East, I could be a little helpful there. But in the last hours they made us draw lots, and my unlucky brother-in-law drew Number One. He wouldn't let me take his place, since my son was present"'—Why, Thomas! So pale, *mein Kind*! I think, per'aps, you should not think about these thing so much—"

My mother ballooned down the hall towards us, in a big rustling brown-and-white striped dress: a bulging tiger with kohl-fringed eyes, and folds of white and gold chiffon scarf flowing from her neck. She had Bear by the arm, his mouth organ stuck obstinately to his lips, blowing very soft and continuous in a wailing hum. She thrust him at Christl.

"Here—take him to his mother, that ironing won't do itself. I hope he won't start to cry again. Are you quite ready, Thomas?" She pushed the hair back from my forehead, almost scalping me.

"'Bye, Zed," piped Bear wanly round the mouth organ. "When's he coming—" But Christl had shut the front door. I pressed the button for the lift.

"Zed! Why does he give you that ridiculous name?"

"I like it," I said absently, still thinking of what Christl had just read to me.

"Your father won't. What an age these lifts do take. Oh, here it is. I wanted you called Maroun, after my father, so of course your father had you called Thomas, after his."

"And Zachary. Z for Zachary. But I'm not any of those names, I'm Zed now. That's what I'm called."

"Don't slouch and scowl like that—my son stands up straight and speaks pleasantly. I don't know what's come over you, Thomas, you're not my sensitive, obedient boy at all, you're downright difficult. All this violence has been very bad for you. Most upsetting."

We reached the ground floor. The lift gates opened, and the hall porter came forward eagerly, as if my mother needed help to cross the lobby.

She smiled at him wistfully, "No, no . . . I can manage. You see I have my son with me again?" Her hand caressed my head with the lightest of touches. "Is the car there?"

"Oh yes, madam."

My mother turned back to me: "Now, when we're outside there will be people with cameras, pushy people, you're not to go running forward as you did yesterday with Christl and Bear. Just smile, and follow me as quickly as you can." In one swift movement she flung up her scarf and settled it like a floating meringue around her head and neck. I winced. Gold and white and pretty—still a bit like Cheetah. She seized my

142

hand. Her little oval nails, almost as small as mine, were painted a fierce shining red.

It was a sparkling sort of day outside, so bright, and brighter still was the barrage of flash, flash as we emerged. There were small cameras and large cameras, and men with big black cameras with BBC and TV and ITV and cable on them; and a trousered woman with long hair said, "*Voilà le petit! Un mot, seulement un mot—*" and knelt down in my path, and my mother yanked me painfully around her, flashing her eyes, and growling through her scarf. I was submerged beneath a brown and white balloon, full of the sweet elusive scent my mother wore, as well as the hot smell of her sweat.

Then we were almost safe in the depths of the chauffeur-driven car, though people on the pavement were surging forward to look in on us as though we were pandas in the Zoo. One man actually got his hand through the half-open window—I just didn't bite him, knowing it wouldn't really please my mother if I did.

The car drove off, flash, flash behind us as we went.

"That's better." She unwound the scarf and forcefully wiped my face with the end of it. "Smuts again *and* on your socks, already. I don't know how you do it. Here—sit up straight and hold these." The car had collected flowers too, from a florist. My mother's were lilies and tiger-lilies, white and orangy brown, they matched her dress. Those she thrust at me were red and white tulips, surrounded softly by something floaty full of little round yellow balls, and very pale silvery-grey leaves. "We'll say you chose them for him yourself, he'll like that."

I thought of throwing them from the window, but the chauffeur had closed it by remote control. I sat looking at them, trying not to see the tulips' redness.

"He's a man," I said sullenly. "He doesn't need flowers. Not in *bed*."

143

Arabi. Under the almond tree. And Omar. In a long wooden box.

The car was drawing up outside the hospital, slow and purring, a serene royal progress. The soft round yellow balls of the mimosa made my eyelids twitch. Snuffle, sneeze, just as we were getting out. There was all that surging forward and flashing again, and this time we stood our ground, my mother well ahead of me, all shy smiles. Flash, flash accompanied us down a polished corridor, nurses beamed from doorways, white forms on trolleys were held up in side passages like a traffic jam to let us pass. Here at last was the ward closed off for the ex-hostages: two policemen on the door, six beds within, and three familiar faces—the older clerk, the Lean Man, and in the farthest bed my Fa: pale, pyjamaed, looking directly at my mother and not at me.

Even the policemen were beaming as some selected journalists were allowed in, and the flashes reflected off the shiny floor. I held my flowers awkwardly, an unhandy wedding page.

"Corney, my darling Corney!" My mother held out her arms, swooping forward in her tiger tent. Striped silk flooded the ward, lilies strewed Fa's bed.

"Leila!"

Flash, flash.

I stood alone, looking down on redness.

"How about one of father and son together now, sir? Aren't you proud of him, lad? Seen the papers?"

Unexpectedly, I was picked up from behind. I kicked backward, outraged, but it was no use: I was being propelled forward, supported as people are who are learning to swim, my arms full of those terrible flowers. The hero's son hovered like a hummingbird, willy-nilly, beside the bed.

For a wild moment I thought of yelling out the truth, and dashing the flowers in his face. The black numbers one and twelve would make a splendid headline.

He knew it. We were so close now that I could have counted his eyelashes, and he was looking at me, unable to avoid me. Our eyes met, and I saw his weren't furious and accusing any longer, not even miserable—but desperate, pleading, like I remember our spaniel's eyes that day we took her to the vet to be put down.

Don't kill me. Don't give me away...

So we really faced each other for the first time since he thrust me from him in the hostage room, and Omar's piece of paper fell to the ground beside me.

But suddenly I wasn't seeing him any more, only Arabi's face that last night when he told me not to take everything too hard. And what was it he said, later on—things I'd closed my mind to at the time, though they came back to me now word for word: "It is easy to break something, but very, very hard to put it together again. It's very important how fathers and sons are with each other, for both of them. It is lifelong. And that means there are always some things better to forget, or not to see."

Then I was looking at Fa, but he had turned aside, was saying to a reporter: "—and my son was offered a chance of freedom, early on, but he chose to stay behind with me—"

He really did believe that. I felt awful about it.

The journalists were closing in again. I thought of Omar and Alley Bear, Feisal and Arabi. "Are you—are you feeling better, Fa?" I asked, putting my silly bunch of red and yellow flowers, silver-leaved, into his hands.

22 THAT WAS ALMOST it: *finis*. I drew a deep deliberate line beneath the word, though I knew I was opting out somehow. I remembered MacArthur's words when he'd first asked me to write about the siege: "—how it all seemed to you at the time... What it did or didn't do for you." And something else, what was it? Oh yes, that I'd struck my earlier teachers as a timid uncertain child. "Perhaps rather crushed at home?" His conclusion, not theirs.

Surely I didn't owe the school any more outpourings? Not these private things—some of which I'd never shared even with Bear.

Bear... Sheikhah. Strange that she and my mother were sisters, Sheikhah so warm and caring, my mother just the opposite. But they were both part of my world, and somehow knowing Omar and Arabi had given me my freedom, left me able to live in that world and find the strength to be myself. They'd had to grow up too, Sheikhah and Leila, though it was hard to imagine their ever being my age. If Sheikhah had made a better job of it than Leila, perhaps that went some way to explain my mother's silly jealousies, her need of the lime-light, her constant griping about other people. And I was proud of her sometimes; she always looked smashing, and all my school friends were bowled over by her charm, though luckily they never heard what she said about them afterwards.

As for my father—I suppose, looking back, our public selves were both comic and sad. Two clowns, each watching the other, afraid of an unrehearsed pratfall. The papers dropped their interest in us after a few days—in a week we rated only a paragraph or so on a back page. And then there we were, face to face with the truth silent between us, and all the wrappings stripped away. As much as I could I took refuge with Christl, Bear and Mustafa—Musti, Bear called him. I even learned to play the mouth organ, and to shift Bear into a major key less upsetting to my mother's nerves.

But I couldn't escape for ever. One evening I went into the drawing room, expecting to find my mother there, returned from shopping. Instead I found my father, sitting alone. It was getting dark, and he hadn't turned the lights on. I thought he'd been crying, just as I'd seen Omar and Arabi cry. What he was crying for seemed so awful, so incurable, that I felt a pain right through me. I mumbled something and was going away, when I felt that I couldn't. I walked in and sat down on the sofa end nearest him, and stared ahead of me. I couldn't think what to say. After a minute or so he said in an unnatural voice, "Had a good day?"

"It was all right. Christl took us out."

"Yes, of course."

There was silence again.

Something prompted me to break it with: "Fa. You know when they—those gunmen—were going to let me go? I went down in the hall with them, and the door opened, and a woman went out, but I couldn't. Just couldn't. I was too scared of the guns. A car backfired, I thought they'd begun shooting at me. I ran back to you. It was a bad moment, and I ran without thinking. Back. I couldn't help myself."

I didn't know if it was wrong to tell him. We sat on, silent, not looking at each other.

"I couldn't help myself," I repeated.

He muttered something indistinct. I thought it was: "I couldn't either."

"Fa."

"Yes?"

I gulped out, "Uncle Omar—you'd have done the same for

147

him if I'd been Alley Bear..." I don't know how I had the nerve to say it.

I thought he said "no" beneath his breath; or perhaps he said nothing.

"And—and he wouldn't have wanted you to feel horrible about it, ever." I couldn't stop now. "It would make what he did so useless, wouldn't it? If you went on feeling horrible, I mean."

I felt I'd overreached myself, wished I'd never opened my mouth.

After a moment he put out his hand and gripped mine. It was quite different from the cold hard grip on our last walk together up Regency Gate.

"Do you remember the last thing he said to me?" he asked huskily. "It was about you... I failed you too, Thomas. You're a fine boy, you did very well as—as Omar said. And I failed you too—"

I was wishing myself anywhere else, but there was nowhere to run to. I muttered something, I don't remember what. Then I had a brainwave: what would Omar have said? 'It's past. Forget it.'

I told Fa. "—that's what Omar would have said."

He sighed. But his voice was stronger when he said, "I must help Sheikhah and Bear—if she'll let me—" He didn't finish his sentence.

I didn't think she would, though I didn't say so. There was something about her almost crazed eagerness to find herself a flat that made me feel she'd guessed. Maybe Omar had said something in his last letter which had made her guess.

"And I must do something for you, too, Thomas—you went through all that, and I haven't—Is there anything special you want?" His voice was shaken again. I couldn't bear it any longer. And I'd heard my mother's footsteps in the hall.

"Would you call me Zed? I like it better. And would you teach me to play chess? There's lots of boys at school play, and I'd like to too. It's something I could join in with—"

The light was clicked on by the door. With infinite relief I heard my mother's voice saying gaily, "All in the dark, you two? I've been wildly extravagant. Smell—it's the latest new scent—don't you think it's delicious? The cost's ridiculous, but one really can't resist." She shed her gloves, bag and parcels—more than new scent, I thought—on to the nearest chair. "What have you done with Bear and Christl, Thomas?"

"They're with Aunt Sheikhah—she's teaching Christl to make a Lebanese thing, in the kitchen."

"Why don't you run along and join them, then?"

I stood up, but my father was saying, "No, no, Leila—I've just promised him his first game of chess. The board's over there in that drawer, Zed, with the chessmen. Could you get them out for us?"

Well. I'd been expected to write something between three and five thousand words...and here instead was Shirley's three-volume novel. *Finis* was the right word, and I'd leave it just where I'd put it. To emphasize it I drew another line underneath the first, and an ornamental squiggle, completing my masterwork with a large clear flourishing ZED. I sat back and looked at the pile of manuscript. Amazing! Specially since I'd no intention of sharing this with a lot of mucky schoolkids; one part of me had known that all along.

MacArthur was going to be livid, and roll out words like "extravagant waste of time". Perhaps he'd believe that I'd simply strung him along to get off schoolwork. He might insist on using what he wanted, and I could see his point without having to make the least effort.

There was just one answer to the problem I was faced with now. However angry MacArthur was, it would be too late for argument.

I stood up and opened the window, uncramping myself

from all that writing, to lean out and breathe the earth-damp air. It was stupendous—with my decision made, that whole task finished and done with, I felt as if some enormous burden, bigger than the task itself, had dropped off my shoulders and rolled away for good. May be something in that shrink racket after all. Now, before picking up my own interesting life again, I felt equal to taking on ten MacArthurs.

I slammed down the window, and turned back into the room, and MacArthur himself was standing by the desk.

"Oh, hell," I said, without thinking.

MacArthur ignored that. He was staring down at the last page, signed with my beautiful curly ZED. "You've finished, I see. Rather too long, isn't it?" He shuffled the pages together, and picked up the whole manuscript. I almost leapt forward to grab it back and tear out of the room with it—but MacArthur had boxed for his University, so it had to be guile.

"I'm taking it home to savage it by chunks." I held out my hand rather too eagerly. He didn't let go of the MS.

"Zed. Long experience has taught me when people are lying." (He has these X-ray sort of eyes, as I've said.) "What are your real intentions, may I ask?"

It was useless lying again, I could see that.

"Tear it up—sir."

His glance was speculative. "Drastic, isn't it? After all that work?"

No sign of outrage. I grew wary, remembering how he had talked me round before. While I hesitated, he asked suddenly, "Those numbers—it wasn't your uncle who drew Number One, was it?" And I said, "No, sir," almost without thinking, and then, "But how did you—" and stopped.

Obvious. There was that one evening I left the MS scattered over the desk, after that painful bit about Omar's death —and next day had found all my papers tidied together, in correct order.

I felt mad as fire with myself and MacArthur—till I caught his sympathetic glance. After all, I hadn't told him how deep in Shirley's advice had taken me, so why shouldn't MacArthur himself have scanned through my work, since it was left lying open for anyone to see? Maybe one part of me really wanted to share those things I'd never told anyone before.

"... can see now it's been an error, from your point of view," he was saying. "But how about the 'savaging by chunks' idea? Needed, anyhow." He smiled, flipping over the thick wad of paper in his hands.

"It's just that none of it—in fact, most of it—" I mumbled inadequately. It was a long while since Zed had felt vulnerable as Thomas—maybe Thomas was still there, battened down inside me; the writing really had taken the lid off something, and I'd never be the same old Zed again.

"Your angle's wrong, too emotional? Perhaps you couldn't have got it down any other way—and now you feel you can't change it? However, there may be ways—" I stiffened. He went on: "If I swear to keep it under lock and key, may I read the whole thing through myself? Your confidence won't be shared with anyone, I promise you."

Put like that, it was impossible to refuse.

"All right. It's just that I don't see what good it can do. None of that can go in any bloody kids' magazine." I was too worried to be tactful.

"Of course not," he said lightly. Cunning old smoothie. But with that MS tucked away beneath his arm, what could I do? "Not a word in it will go anywhere without your permission. Come and see me after school on Friday, and we'll talk more about it then. Now I'm off—late home as it is. And so will you be."

He jerked his head towards the door, and I followed him from the room. We went in silence down the corridor, and out into the bluish dusk. MacArthur stowed my manuscript in a briefcase on the back of his Thunderbolt, pulled on his

151

crash helmet, and kicked the engine into life.

"Thanks for your co-operation, Zed."

Sitting in the bus I decided that he was bound to have some spectacular accident, roaring off in that rakish way at his advanced age. Anybody might pick my masterwork off the sidewalk, and even publish it whole in the evening paper— and I wouldn't get a penny for the scoop.

When Friday came I was feeling better and more hopeful. If Thomas was surfacing inside Zed, at least he was under control. And sharing my family skeletons with someone as detached as MacArthur was a relief. For so long they'd been rattling about for my benefit alone—and if you could trust anyone, you could trust MacArthur. But later that day I began to get stomachache; psychosomatic, the shrinks would say.

I went over to MacArthur's own study after tea, and found him sitting in an easy chair, my MS spread around him on the floor. At one glance I saw that some pages were already xeroxed, and others slashed here and there in red.

"Oh, it's you. Come along in, Zed. If you'd like to brew us up some coffee, make use of that machine over there."

I was glad of something practical to do. While I was fidgeting about, fetching brown sugar from his cupboard, and keeping an eye on the coffee, MacArthur asked: "How's your cousin Ali Baha these days?"

"He's surviving. Though they're pretty poor. Uncle Omar hadn't thought much about dying—all his money was the firm's."

"I thought Arabs were so hot on family obligations?" He sounded rather like my mother.

"Depends on the Arab and the obligations, sir."

"Enlighten me."

"You see—my mother's family would help, but the conditions were that Aunt Sheikhah should go home, and bring him up as a Maronite, and she won't because of Uncle Omar. So that's out."

"And his father's family?"

"Much the same thing, sir—in reverse. They never accepted her because she'd been a Maronite, at least they were never nice to her, not at all."

"But the boy's a Muslim, isn't he?"

"They both are. And Bear's grandfather wrote two years ago to say he'd take him into his household, now he was old enough to leave his mother, and bring him up as his own son for Omar's sake, however much Omar had upset and disgraced his family by his marriage."

"I never guessed the Middle East was so nineteenth-century Victorian."

"No, sir—and the old man's a Mullah now, you see, as well."

"And so your aunt wasn't prepared to comply?"

"Oh yes, she was all ready for the self-sacrifice bit, crying and packing Bear's trunk, and buying him a locket for her portrait—only Bear scotched it all. He wrote a letter to his grandfather saying he'd insulted both his mother and his father's memory, and crept out and posted it when she wasn't looking. So that was that, and Uncle Omar's brothers all rejoiced like anything, and gathered for the pickings like a flock of bl— ravens, sir."

"I'm beginning to like the sound of Bear. He lost out badly, poor chap, didn't he? And he must feel rather cut off over here."

It was a reproach I often made myself. I guessed MacArthur was wondering why my own family weren't helping more—or perhaps, having read the MS, he knew why already. I said, hurried and rather guiltily, "Aunt Sheikhah's so proud, she won't take too much help from my father. Is this coffee strong enough, sir?" I carried a cup over to him.

"Strong? It looks like mud."

"Shall I make some more?"

"Leave it, leave it—it can't kill us, for once." He stirred it fretfully, and took a sip as though it might. "Anyway, you'll be glad to know I agree—in the main—with your judgment: most of what came pouring out is entirely for yourself. That siege explains quite a lot about you that always seemed fairly baffling to me before, Zed. I expected you to write something interesting—I didn't realise we were inviting such catharsis."

I made a mental note to look that one up. MacArthur expects his English class to understand him. "Now look, there are slices we can use—here, and here, see?" He demonstrated, picking up one xeroxed page after another, then pointing out paragraphs on other pages marked in red. "Extracts, a linking commentary—with bits of background stuff thrown in."

I must have groaned, for he looked at me satirically.

"That's all right, Zed, I've arranged most of it already, and once you've okayed everything I'll tie it all up myself."

"Thanks for your co-operation, sir."

He looked at me over his half-moon glasses like an angry badger, which can unnerve you if you let it, so I added quickly, "Can I xerox the photos and captions from that colour supplement, for you to use as well?"

He shook his head. "But suppose we use those original snaps of your 'Arabi's'?" He looked indescribably cunning. "The ones you kept?"

"Sorry, sir. I did destroy them in the end." (As a matter of fact I had them on me then, wondering if I'd let him see them.) I met his unbelieving gaze with my most polished look of innocence. After a moment he laughed.

"All right, Zed—you win. Perhaps I shouldn't have asked. Look through what I've chosen as soon as you can, and let me know if there's anything you object to. This coffee's dreadful—fetch me some beer from that cupboard. And since we're well outside school hours, try some yourself."

I was on my way out, feeling more at ease and clutching my ravaged MS with the xeroxed pages and the supplement under one arm, when I fell in with Tosh Perkins, sloping by from the canteen, with his usual myopic look of not knowing where he is. The pebble glasses didn't help. Tosh always reminds me of a goldfish that's been too long in an uncleaned tank: that way they have of sloping to one side, weighed down by fuzz about the scales. His real friends tell me he has unsuspected charm—it's like keeping newts, they grow on you. But in my view Tosh can only communicate with the real world through a camera lens. His special talent gave me an idea. One of my most inspired flashes.

"Are you busy just now?" I asked.

His head weaved about a bit—he might have been trying to find an answer on the wall. I sympathised, really, knowing my own reactions if someone asks that sort of open question.

"Well. Yes. No," he mumbled, not too forthcomingly. Though Tosh never does forthcome, except about grainy film or too much contrast, or something like that.

"Buy you a roll of film, if you'll show me how to print from a print, and enlarge it," I offered. "Would that be difficult?"

I could see him thinking. Tosh's face is even more like a goldfish's when he starts to churn up the thinktank.

"Two rolls," he said finally.

"OK, done. Can you show me now?"

"If you like. And if I can have those rolls of film tomorrow."

We went along to the darkroom, and Tosh fumbled with the enlarger and other mysteries, while I brought out the photos I'd taken from Arabi's pocket all those years ago, and placed them ready. I really had meant to show them to MacArthur, though after that there might have been no controlling him in his lust for magazine fodder. Not even Alley Bear had seen them. But showing them to Tosh was as impersonal as putting them before a camera lens.

"These your peculiar relations?" he said amicably.

"Stuff it." I showed him the whites of my eyes, and he said, "All right, all right" in mock panic. "Don't hit the enlarger", and he picked up the prints almost as tenderly as I'd put them down, and began measuring them up for size.

We finished late. The boarders had gone over to the other house for supper, and most of the place was locked up before we left, parting at the bus stop, because Tosh goes home by underground. Even his company would have been welcome. I was feeling fairly rough—the effect of those photographs. They'd been a long while in their old hiding-place, and it had been a long while since I'd looked at them so closely—those small black and white squares with power to resurrect that night of noise and fire, red flowers beneath an almond tree, the smell of cold wet earth, light reflecting off open eyes.

The bus jolted along with infuriating slowness till it reached our stop, and by that time enthusiasm for my fine idea had almost gone. It seemed about as sane as Tosh, even MacArthur's original scheme was sanity beside it. In fact, I almost discarded my whole plan. My father and I had been responsible for some things, all right—but not for Bear writing that letter to his grandfather.

I let myself into our flat as quietly as possible; even so my young brother heard me. He came out of his room—the one Bear used to have—like a tornado. In fact, he's very like Bear, except that he's bigger for his age, and angrier, like a little bull. He's called Maroun, my mother got her way that time.

"Zed, Zed, you're late again—I've got something to show you, I went a walk with Friedl, I got some sweets. In the park I got some flowers—come an' see?"

"Oh shut it, you." He's so big for six and a half, he's exhausting. Then I relented. "Come on, then. Show me."

He led the way into his room, and shut the door behind us. The sweets were by his bed—Smarties—but the flowers were in his blue satchel, hidden behind the curtain. Pulled up by the roots, clump of mud and all. Heaven knows how he'd managed it without Friedl seeing (she's Swiss, and looks after him). But he's a terrible thief. Accomplished.

"Pretty?"

"You mustn't do that," I told him. "Park keeper will be after you. And Friedl. How are you going to keep and hide them?" They were blatantly scarlet tulips.

"You keep them for us," he said confidently. "In your room."

"Thanks very much." But I took an earthenware pot from his shelf, and stuck the flowers in it, mud and all.

"What's that?" he asked, staring at the MS under my arm.

"Homework. And that's quite enough from you."

He smiled sunnily. He knows when he's gone too far.

"Have a Smartie, Zed?"

"I don't need chocolate any more."

He looked puzzled—didn't latch on to the idea of not needing chocolate at any time. "Go along to Friedl," I told him and picked up the pot of flowers and carried them to my own room. My father heard me this time. He put his head out of the drawing room, where I could hear the television in full blast.

"You're very late, Zed. Didn't you want to see that programme—it's almost over?"

It was a 'match of the day' sort of thing, and we usually watched it together.

"Sorry, but I've brought back some more work." His eyes shifted to the tulips, and I saw a question forming, so I said hurriedly, "It's a special project." Whoever coined that one thought up a really useful word.

He looked disappointed. "They're giving you almost too many, this term. Your O levels were first class, you could have some free time now."

"I'll be through with it soon—next week, anyway."

I escaped into my room, feeling a bit guilty about letting MacArthur see the whole MS. The curtains were undrawn, the blue hazy light reflecting off the panes. I put the flowers on my table by the window, and they glimmered against the shine, doubling their image, startlingly red.

"Oh, all right, then—if that's a hint, you win," I said aloud to empty air, half ashamed of talking as if Arabi could hear me. I cleared everything else off the table, then spread out the pages from the colour supplement, side by side with Tosh's handiwork. I skipped through the article till I found what I was looking for: the name of Feisal's stepfather. (I'd looked up his Embassy's address in the school telephone directory.) Then I sat down and began to write my letter.

23 MY PARENTS WENT went off to some conference in
Brussels midweek, which fitted in very nicely with
my own arrangements. Saturday was a fine day, and
I set out early to walk some of the way. There'd been no
answer to my letter, but I hadn't really expected one. At
eleven o'clock, I'd said, and on the steps of the Albert Memorial, facing the Albert Hall. I'd chosen it because it was
central, and anyway the whole project had begun at Consort's, so the Memorial seemed a fitting place for it to end. At
least the old boy himself might keep a watchful eye on me. I
bit my nails now and then—but I wasn't really nervous: not
me, Zed.

Bear had been furious with me—first, because he'd wanted
us to go out for the day, and then because I wouldn't tell him
anything.

"You'll get over it," I told him on the phone. "Tell you
later, if it works out."

"I don't see why you need act so mysterious," he grum-
bled. "And I was keeping this Saturday. Now there's nothing
to do."

"Take Cliff to a film," I suggested.

"I'm giving *you* a black eye," said Bear's distant voice. "Can
you feel it?"

"Keep it for Cliff. With my love. Now I must go. It's all in
your interest, too," I added, and rang off.

In spite of walking, and busing, and then walking again, I was
ten minutes early, so I made a slight detour and reached the
Memorial through the meadowy bit on the Consort's left. I

sat on the steps facing the Hall, put my carefully truncated manuscript down beside me, and waited. The steps were cold, and I was glad I'd made myself tidier than usual in my school blazer. The sun was shining and there was a cool little wind. People came and went past me; mostly foreigners who stood staring at old Albert, or climbed up to have a closer look at him. Sometimes they took snaps of each other standing by the huge sculpted animals and people at the four corners of the Memorial's foot.

For twenty minutes I waited, and nothing happened. I began to feel deflated—probably he wouldn't come. About eleven a car had driven up and stopped at the side of the road just below me and opposite the entrance to the Hall. There were three men in it, who sat there idly, not getting out. Perhaps they were waiting to buy tickets for a concert. I didn't know when the Box Office opened, maybe it was late on Saturdays. A quarter of an hour later a second car drove up: chauffeur-driven, a woman sitting by herself in the back.

I began to feel certain Feisal wouldn't come. I was wasting my time—I'd wait another few minutes, then go. I rearranged the manuscript by my side with the two big enlargements on top of it. It was theatrical perhaps—but it did identify me. When I looked up, the woman was out of her car, talking to the chauffeur. The other car was empty. Its occupants were climbing the lower steps towards me. Halfway up they divided, two to the right, one to the left; walking at an angle which took them higher than my level, they cleared the corner sculptures and disappeared beyond them.

The woman wasn't buying tickets either. She came walking straight up towards me, with an air of gentle determination. She was tall and graceful in a narrow black coat, with some filmy stuff around her neck like my mother often wore. The sun shone on gleaming dark hair, pulled into a heavy knot. As she came closer to me, blurred features resolved themselves into a familiar face . . . those large dark eyes—

160

I got to my feet. So Feisal's mother had come instead.

She halted three or four steps below me. I stood there feeling horribly embarrassed. She looked composed and slightly accusing. She gave a quick glance at the manuscript, with the enlarged photos on top of it. I saw her start. Or wince.

"You are Thomas Amsterel?"

I nodded. I couldn't speak.

"So it was you who wrote that letter to my son, and sent the little snapshot of us together? Why? What do you want of us?" She sounded hostile.

From the corners of my eyes I caught a glimpse of swift movement. The three men from the first car had returned from the Memorial, and were approaching us. Right hands inside their overcoats, they came to a halt just above us on the steps. Dark moustaches, narrow unfriendly eyes.

So she'd brought along her bodyguard.

A sweeping gesture of her hands showed them to me. She said "Don't try to run away," and moved right up to me till she was looking into my face. I stumbled back, appalled by what she seemed to be thinking, and with a strong sense of "I have been here before"—those hidden guns! Either my legs gave, or I tripped on the step, for I went down, floundering, snatching up the manuscript. Quick as a flash, one of her men pounced on the fallen photographs.

"Who has put you up to this—your parents?"

I sat there, stupidly nursing the manuscript, wind blowing my hair into my eyes, and half-blinded by sun. People walked past us, and up the steps, glancing at us as they went. What would they do if I shouted for help? Probably look away and walk faster.

"It's—it's not—You've got it all wrong," I stuttered.

I began to struggle up, and one of her men caught me by the arm. I pulled free, but he still hovered too close for comfort.

"We've been here for some time—he's spoken to no one. We've checked round the back, and we find nothing suspicious," said one of the others in Arabic. "We think he's alone."

She answered in the same tongue: "That means nothing. He might have meant to take my son somewhere else, they may be waiting there."

"But you've got it all *wrong*," I repeated, panicstricken, and her eyes sharpened, and she said, "Ah—so you're really fluent in Arabic, yes? That part was no lie, at least. Is this revenge or blackmail—or kidnapping? Speak, you!"

I was so stunned that I didn't know what to answer. I began stuttering again, "I—I—I—"

Perhaps my state of shock seemed genuine. For the first time she looked a bit uncertain. It steadied me, and I seized the chance to say, "It's—it's nothing like that! Please can't I speak to you a minute alone?" I couldn't get my thoughts clear with those thugs breathing down the back of my neck.

There was a rapid explosion of Arabic from one of the men; I only caught a few words, and her easy reply, "Fan out, then—he can't get away from three of you, surely!" To me she said: "Wait."

We waited, while they regrouped themselves, one above us on the steps, the others to our right and left, just out of earshot. In fact, they jumped to obey her.

I thought there was a touch of steel about Feisal's mother, beneath that filmy scarf. In the supplement photograph she looked like a timid gazelle; now it was easier to understand why she'd first married a terrorist—even one whose views she disagreed with—and then a high-ranking diplomat. *He* looked tough enough, and tough he must be to represent the top toughies of his country's government.

"They won't hear you now." She sat down, spreading her skirts about her. I sat too, awkwardly, and suddenly she gave me a teasing, almost comradely smile. "Are you scared?"

"*No.*" Yet I was, although not so much now, since like this she seemed more the woman in Arabi's photograph: Arabi's wife, holding his child by the hand.

"What is it you want to tell me?"

"I never imagined your son would show you my letter— You *would* think it was for all the wrong reasons!" It sounded lame. She just looked at me, and I began again, "You see, he—Arabi—"

"Who? Oh—yes. You are speaking of my—my first husband, Javed." She bent her head, and stared at the step.

"That was the name he was using—And I was only eight —They shot my uncle—he was the only one killed. My father was there too, but—Anyway, Arabi was very good to me, when things—when they were worst. He was—kind." Limp as well as lame. I swallowed. The words were coming out all wrong, there was so much, how could I get it through to her? She was sitting with bent head still, appearing to listen.

"He, Arabi—Javed knew he would be killed, I think. He was trying to make me face things for myself, to understand the—the clash of things and how nothing bad lasts for ever, so not to be afraid. He tried not to show it but he was upset too. Miserable, and—" I faltered.

"Go on," she said, not looking up.

"My uncle was shot because of me. He took my—someone else's place—it was horrible." I paused.

"I can see—yes." She sounded kinder.

"He had a son—Ali Baha. My cousin. I'm half Arab, you see. Uncle Omar always carried his photo everywhere. I told him—Arabi—that, and he showed me yours with Feis- —your son's. The one I put in my letter to show it was real. He—he was thinking of you both a lot, that night. He cried. About Feisal. Oh—and about you," I added quickly.

She made a sudden movement, and a slight sound. Her neck was bent, her face was hidden from me. I went on,

163

hurrying it out, "He said you hadn't understood—I mean, why he acted as he did. And he was very worried for—for Feisal's future. He said he would destroy the photos so that nobody would trace you both, but he hadn't, when he died. Perhaps he couldn't bear to, after all. Anyway, someone traced you later, didn't they?"

"You are saying he—Javed—gave them to *you*?" She was almost whispering.

"Oh no. It was after— He was shot, you see. And I remembered what he said... He was so good to me," I repeated dully. "I couldn't let them—the police or the army —find them, if he had them still. So I took them. Afterwards. I knew they were in his shirt pocket. No one else had found them first."

She raised her head then. "A child your age? To do a thing like that? But no, it is not possible!"

I felt stung. "It is! They took us all outside, and they—the gunmen—were dumped down as if—dumped on the grass, near us. It was just getting light, no one saw me. There was a flowering tree, he was beneath it—" I was willing her to believe me. "Red petals," I said, "I thought it was all red petals—over him, but it wasn't—I took the photos—I hid them afterwards. And then I kept them. A sort—a sort of talisman. And to remember him by. You see, though they were on different sides, he was so like my—my Uncle Omar." I had run out of breath, my hands were shaking. Hers too.

Her voice shook, as well. "But why now, why—That letter—you never thought of that yourself?" She sounded as if she would be glad to pin something on to someone else.

"I did! It was that Sunday supplement article—you must have known about it, surely? But I didn't think of writing to Feisal until—" I looked down at my manuscript, a bit grubby and tattered by this time. "Here," I thrust it at her—into her lap. She sat staring at it, not touching it.

"What is this, then?"

"It's—my house master at school made me write about the siege for—for a sort of big school project. Oh, I've taken out some chunks, and the end part too, they were just for me —But—if you'd just read it—I was going to give it to him, Feisal—the big photos are for him, too. Just to show him what sort of man Arabi—his father was—In case Feisal felt he'd done something terrible, and he had, and yet—" I struggled helplessly with words, it was so hard to explain. Still, I'd started it. I had to try.

"They both lost out the same way, didn't they? Feisal and Alley B.—my cousin, Ali Baha. Both their fathers shot. They're the same age, almost. I thought they could be friends, maybe." I remembered Arabi—and the tough-looking new husband. I said cruelly, wanting to hurt her, "Feisal doesn't look very happy, anyway. Is he? And Alley —Ali Baha isn't, really. He's so cut off from—from his roots, over here. He doesn't really know what he's missing. I'm only half Arab, but I *know* . . . I've often been back there, to my mother's family. Well, Uncle Omar's family hasn't helped him, because—Oh, forget it. This was all a silly rotten idea."

My forehead was sweating. Cripes! And she'd thought it was all for blackmail! I shouldn't have put those pompous phrases in my letter about Arab obligations; high-flown stuff, but it had sounded good at the time. I curled up inside at the thought.

"Your letter never reached my son," she was saying slowly. "Since it was sent care of my husband to the Embassy, he opened it. He was furious, he would come himself, he would send—" She looked down towards the Hall. "But because it was to do with Javed—your Arabi—I persuaded him it was for me to come, and I would be safe enough, here in the open . . . with these—" she glanced round at her bodyguard.

"No, I don't think we can just forget it. Come," she said, and stood up briskly. "We'll take you back with us now."

165

I didn't like the sound of that, or of the husband.

I stood up too. "You can't kidnap *me* with a foreign body-guard! Not *here*. The police—"

Although I'd swear she'd been almost crying, she looked amused.

"See there—" she pointed. Down by the Hall a Panda car was half hidden by the hoardings.

"*We* are not bandits. All is most discreetly and diplomatically arranged. Come!"

I felt more embarrassed still, I could feel my face turning fiery red. So he'd thought it bad enough to call in the police. Worse and worse. But there was nothing for it. She was beckoning her men to follow, and they closed in behind me, while she took me by the arm and drew me along with her. I went without protest, feeling no end of a fool, inwardly cursing MacArthur and dreading what my family would say. A sprint for freedom could only lead to public disaster.

As we descended the steps, the Panda drove out from its position, and pulled in ahead of the two other cars. One policeman got out, leaving another at the wheel.

I stood by the chauffeur, scowling at my shoes, while she spoke to her bodyguard, and they spoke to the police. It seemed to last for ever. There was a lot of nodding and gesturing and—at last—some open grinning. The policeman got back into the Panda, and the woman turned to me. "Get in."

At that, one of her bodyguard protested.

She said coolly, "You can search him if you like, late though you leave it. Maybe he has a knife, but I don't think he looks like a desperado."

So I had to suffer the indignity. They made a thorough job of frisking me, and I forced myself to stand quietly, red-faced, as passers-by stared curiously while two of the heavily-moustached men in mackintoshes gave me a thorough going over. Inwardly, I was threatening them with all sorts of legal action and illegal violence. It was humiliating to see the two policemen sit there grinning. Free country, indeed.

At last it was over. The Panda drove off ahead of us, and we followed, like the middle of a sandwich.

"Where are we going? To your Embassy?"

She shook her head, looking away from me and out of the window. "No. To our present home."

We didn't speak, after that. She still sat turned away. She'd taken a handkerchief from her bag and was dabbing at her eyes. I felt fiercely glad if I had made her cry.

It came as something of a shock to find that her home was one of the larger Regency Gate houses, so close to the Company building of Uncle Omar's family firm. As we got out of her car, surrounded by police and bodyguards, I pointed it out to her, wondering how she felt about it. Just to look at it churned me up inside.

"You know that was where it all happened?"

She stared at me blankly. I couldn't tell if she'd known or not. I said: "It's where they both died—Omar and Arabi. They were so alike in some ways—and they died in the same way, blasted full of bullet holes. And they were people who ought to have lived." I'd make myself cry, in a minute. As for her—I was glad to see how she had to fumble, to get her key in the front door lock.

24 THEY PUT ME in a large room on the first floor and left me there. The police treated me as if I were eight years old again, and I heard them talking and laughing with the bodyguard, out on the landing. I put my head round the door, and said, "I want to see my lawyer," and that made them laugh even more.

"Your Dad can decide about that, son. You just sit down there quietly and wait, like a good boy."

"Have you sent for him? It won't be any use—he's at a conference and—"

But they wouldn't listen to me, told me nothing, and shut the door on me again. I looked out of the window, and decided not to jump.

The room was very quiet, and I'd plenty of time to meditate on being held prisoner for the second time in Regency Gate. It was an expensive, dull sort of room. Sheeny Persian rugs, very rich-looking, on the walls. A few lilies, in a chinese vase. Large bowls of cobalt blue, with floral scrolls, just like the ones my grandmother had in her Lebanese house. Everything was ultra-clean and still. I thought about Feisal, and wondered if he was ultra-clean and quiet too. There was nothing to read, unless you count newspapers in various foreign languages, as well as the *New York Herald Tribune* and the *Financial Times*. I didn't want to try any of them. I just sat, chewing my nails.

After what seemed like a long while, and probably was, a man came in and began shouting at me, waving his hands about. He didn't introduce himself, but I recognised him anyway, from that colour supplement. Feisal's stepfather. It was rather unpleasant, and I had time to think that no wonder the Middle East was in a mess if they all shouted like that in Embassies. He had my letter to Feisal in his hand, and he kept slapping it between shouts. What it all added up to was that that phrase of mine about Arab honour and obligations had really got his goat.

"Money, money, is this what you wanted?" he kept saying, without giving me a chance to speak. Each time he opened his mouth there was a flash from his solid gold back teeth. I'd thought that phrase dignified, rather well put— something that might have earned nods of approval from MacArthur in class. Now I could see just what it looked like. At last he stopped shouting, but nothing I stammered out was any use. He just stared at the badge on my blazer, asked which school I came from, and my Headmaster's name, and trundled out, giving off dark suspicious glances as he went.

There was another long wait, and then I heard a taxi drawing up outside. I peered out to see who it was, and there was MacArthur getting out, looking extremely sour with his worst badger face. Our Head must have rung him. My spirits rose and fell at the same time—fell because I knew he didn't like his family weekends disturbed, and rose because even Feisal's stepfather might have met his match. I was quaking a good deal, what with all that had happened since eleven, and no lunch. After seven years Thomas was really back hand in hand with Zed.

It was still some while before I was ushered downstairs by one of those creeps of bodyguards. I'd heard the Panda drive off just before, and hoped that was a better sign. The creep pushed me inside what seemed to be the drawing room and went away. It was a very large room, with a highly polished floor and more of those rugs on the walls. I didn't really notice it much, having more important things on my mind—Feisal's mother and stepfather; and MacArthur too, sitting there very much at his ease. There was quite a good feeling in the room,

Thomas's resurrected antennae told me that, and I managed to stop quaking—outwardly, at least.

MacArthur merged well with diplomacy, and delicate china and silver and all that. They had coffee, and coffee cake too—my mouth watered just looking at it. But I didn't have time to look long, because MacArthur was speaking, and when that happens he likes your full attention.

"Hah, Zed—I wish you could be persuaded to confine your more unusual activities to the weekdays, my dear boy, especially when your parents are away," he said, badgering smoothly at me over his half-moon glasses.

"I'm sorry, sir." I really was. And for myself. "But that letter was only meant for—for Feisal. I just thought it would be nice for him and Alley B—Ali Baha to meet. Sort of."

Feisal's stepfather's big fat face crinkled up round the eyes, and suddenly he let out a guffaw worse than his shouting. If he didn't slap MacArthur on the back it was only because they were separated by cream jugs, etc. You can see why Middle East politics are so unstable. Ganging up and then unganging faster than in Europe. I decided then and there that I'd chuck my mother's idea of sending me to the American University at Beirut. My father would be glad to hear I was settling for Redbrick or Oxbridge, if I got that far.

I was just adding honestly: "And I did think they might help Bear later on to—" when I caught MacArthur's full frontal frown, and shut up fast.

Feisal's mother stood up then, and beckoned me over to her. She looked gentle and smaller in her husband's presence—almost timid. The steeliness had disappeared.

"Zed—please come over here. I think we should apologise to you, poor fellow. We have quite misunderstood you, it seems. I am sorry too that Feisal isn't here today."

An apology hardly seemed enough for all I'd been through, but MacArthur's right eye closed for a second, then the lid shot up again, and he was once more giving his interpretation

170

of a crusty and responsible house master. So I mumbled none too graciously, "Oh, that's all right." The last thing I wanted now to round off the day was an actual meeting with Feisal.

"Would you like some tea—or coffee? You would?"

She rang a bell, and a white-jacketed manservant appeared and was sent away to fetch fresh coffee, and some vile little postage-stamp sandwiches stuck together with greyish-pink glue. I decided straight away for the coffee cake.

"—and we have telephoned your cousin Ali's mother," she was saying. "Poor woman, she was quite, quite horrified."

So was I. "She's so proud, Aunt Sheikhah. She—she'll absolutely slaughter me." It wasn't a very fair portrait of Aunt Sheikhah, but I thought it best to lay the slaughtering on with a trowel.

"So? We must put that right, then. I have invited her to lunch with us here next week."

"But—but did she accept?"

"Oh, yes. We had a long talk on the telephone, and already what comes out is that we know her husband's family quite well. Once we have met her, and talked more together, then perhaps my Feisal and her Ali Baha should meet...it is perhaps ordained...so strange, they should be almost of an age, and—" She looked towards the window, and left the sentence unfinished.

I could see from her husband's face who would do the ordaining—or otherwise.

"We have just looked through your work, a little." This time she glanced at my tatty manuscript, that was now lying on MacArthur's knees. "It is truly sad. Not always easy to follow, because—I hope you won't be hurt, it is disjointed here and there."

I caught MacArthur's sardonic eye, and murmured, "I took out quite a few bits, private ones. It got chopped about, rather."

Later, she gave me her hand, ultra-gracious, as we said

171

goodbye. My mother would have told me to kiss it, but I didn't. She wasn't nearly good enough for Arabi. I only hoped that Feisal was. His stepfather clapped me on the back, and said almost jovially that he daresaid he'd be seeing me again some time. His eyes were tiny, like narrow chips of coal; he looked as though he could have run the PLO in his spare time and not even noticed it.

In the taxi, I said: "Thanks, sir. However did you manage it?"

"Fortunately I managed to convince them that we were dealing here with one of those peculiar scholars who are also, by some freak of nature, natural imbeciles."

"Thank you very much, sir."

"Any time. What were you really hoping for, from that remarkable epistle, Zed? And why, in the name of heaven, boy, didn't you consult me first?"

"It—it just seemed such a good idea at the time, and—er—" I watched him sideways—"I'd told you I destroyed the photographs, sir. Sorry about it."

"Yes. Well. We'll forget that."

"It—it happened really because I met Tosh Perkins just after I'd been working on the MS with you."

"Tosh Perkins?" MacArthur closed his eyes for a moment, with a pained expression, muttered, "Give me strength," opened his eyes and asked, "How many more people like you and Tosh are involved in this?"

I thought coupling me with Tosh was a bit harsh, even for MacArthur, but I couldn't really quibble just then.

"Oh, no one else, sir," I said hastily. "Tosh just helped me make the enlargements—he didn't know anything about it otherwise. One thing sort of led to another. It was a feeling that Feisal and Bear might meet, and if maybe they were friends it would sort of wipe out the past, somehow—and do something in a way for Arabi and Omar. I felt Feisal's stepfather might know Bear's grandfather or uncles—and he might—sort of—"

"Put some diplomatic pressure on them? Sort of, you would say?"

"Yes, sir."

"Hmmm—Quite an ingenious notion."

He stared out of the taxi window thoughtfully. His shoulders were shaking. Suddenly, he began to chuckle.

"What's funny, sir?"

"You, Zed. Your letter. What they thought. I was just visualising your esteemed and pompous father lurking in the Flower Walk with a bunch of armed men disguised as Canterbury bells, waiting to execute some form of belated vengeance on that woman's son!" Snuffle, snuffle. "Luckily I was able to convince them he was sufficiently well-heeled to dispose of the alternative explanation." He was positively howling now, rubbing his hands together with glee. "This has been worth your wasting my spare time . . . I wouldn't have missed it for the world."

I couldn't raise a smile.

"Oh Zed, Zed—take that priggish expression off your face, my dear boy. I fear you're becoming rather a prig, you know. Let this be a lesson to you—it's highly dangerous manipulating other people's lives: it requires a degree of humility that you haven't got. I must say, I rather liked Thomas—perhaps you've suppressed him for too long? Perhaps you should let him out for an airing, what's it these analysts say—integrate him? And what will your cousin think of your arrangements? Perhaps he won't want to see his grandfather again, eh? And specially not through the son of a man who helped to kill his father?"

I felt cross and misunderstood.

"Arabi never meant to—I think I'll get out here, sir, if you don't mind."

"I do mind. I'm perfectly aware of what you're thinking. It's all my fault, for making you write out your experiences.

Mea culpa, Zed—*mea culpa*, a little. But whatever you learnt from the tragedies of your uncle and—er—his opponent, surely you at least learnt that nothing's ever entirely one person's fault? Don't end up pompous like your respected father, I do beg you. This afternoon has been high comedy. I've enjoyed it, even if you haven't—can't you even wring one smile from it?"

Reluctantly, I smiled. I even began to laugh—it was rather funny, when you came to think of it. MacArthur was really doubled up. After all, he had saved me from a good deal of trouble, to say the least. I was just beginning to think he was really on the level after all, when he sobered up suddenly, and said in his most badgery way, "That letter. *Very* badly expressed. From one of my own pupils too—and after all those essays. *A propos*—Mr. Shirley has asked me to remind you that he is looking forward to your French essay on Proust."

Alley Bear wasn't even mildly grateful.

"What did you want to do a thing like that for?" he wailed at me down the telephone some days later. "Mother went to lunch there yesterday, she had to, after what you did. She bought herself some filthy scent and hideous clothes, we'll be living on cheese rind all next week, I should think. And just to chat up some super-glossy thugs who killed my father."

"Listen, for cripes sake, they didn't—and I didn't mean—"

"What's worse, she seems not to mind them too much, and she says Omar would have approved of what you did, and now I've got to give up next Saturday to meet this twit son, he sounds awful, he does lessons alone with an Imam, and goes out in a chauffeur-driven car, I can't think what Cliff will say—"

"What the hell's it got to do with Cliff?" I was taken aback by his onslaught, but glad Sheikhah thought Omar would have approved, anyway.

"He was coming to a film next Saturday, you said ask him.

Things were just getting better, a whole gang of us were going. Now I'm stuck. You'll have to come too, Zed—I won't meet that twit alone. I bet his Imam's like my grandfather, and he'll probably recite the Koran all through tea—"

"OK, if you want me to." My spirits sank. "You'll like Feisal anyway, if he's like his Dad."

"You're mad, Zed. He'll be foul, I don't know what you're on about. His foul Dad killed mine. You were so shit-scared of those guns, you'd have chummed with a gorilla if it gave you chocolate. I thought you *liked* Omar."

"I did. I loved him. I—I'll give you something to read I wrote about him and Arabi—"

"That's enough," said Bear. "Think I want to read your soggy outpourings? It's for three o'clock Saturday. They're sending a car for me. He'll be waiting at his home, we're to go a walk in the Park—no, *really!*—and then back to their foul house for tea. Meet you there for *sure?*"

"*W'allahi*—I won't let you down," I said, trying to pacify him.

"You'd better not. I say, I knocked Cliff down first—and I've just thought of something...Well, *w'allahi*—see you Saturday."

He rang off.

25 SATURDAY WAS ONE of those changeable days: heavy clouds, thundery with white fringed edges, laying the dust with sudden tremendous rainfall, then rolling away to show patches of cobalt blue. When the sun came out, London steamed. Everything smelt very strongly of itself, and the buses rolled by splashing ankles with mud and water as they passed.

My family had only returned from Brussels midweek, Friedl had held the fort till then. I saw no need to let them in on my activities, though it seemed almost too much to hope that they wouldn't hear of them some time. MacArthur had kept aloof, after fending off the police, which was decent of him. But I wasn't sure of keeping Aunt Sheikhah quiet for ever. She'd already rung me to ask if the Embassy car couldn't pick me up too? And I said no, no—my mother would ask questions, and *no*, I wouldn't let Bear down, and *W'allahi*, yes I'd be there by three.

I went by underground. It brought me out near the Park itself, which meant I could walk along beside it and look down Regency Gate—and be there by the house quickly enough when the car came back with Bear. I had to loiter a bit, because I was early. The Park trees were very green, great wafts of lime strong on the thundery air. There were trees in the garden on my left, too, I could see their tops over a high wall. It was a minute or so before it dawned on me that this was the Company's garden, that was the Company building at an angle on the nearest corner, and some of the branches must belong to the trees that had been in bloom seven years ago.

I waited on the corner, not wanting to be there, and keeping my eyes from sliding sideways towards the portico, the columns, the dusty half-moon entrance. I wondered if there were still bullet holes in the marble, or if they'd been filled in and smoothed over long ago. There was no one outside the portico, perhaps they kept their security guard penned inside, these days.

The traffic flowed past by the Park, and up and down Regency Gate. I kept my eyes on the Victorian-pillared entrance of Feisal's home. At two minutes to three the door opened, and someone a bit taller than Bear but skinnier came out on to the steps to wait. Feisal stood with his hands in his pockets and his shoulders almost hunched up to his ears. He glanced behind him now and then, and I thought he wanted to bolt back inside. I had more dismal thoughts about my whole idea. The MS was in a leather bag slung over my shoulder. I couldn't imagine why I'd brought it along. It wasn't likely we'd be sitting like three crows in a row on a park bench while I read from it.

A largish car was coming slowly up the street now, bang on time. Clockwork chauffeur. I kept my promise to Bear and walked rapidly to meet it. I was there at the foot of the steps when Bear got out—he didn't wait for the chauffeur to come round and open the door, he just tumbled out in a hurry, scowling and embarrassed. He must have won a battle with Aunt Sheikhah over his clothes, because he was wearing some patched and faded jeans, and his favourite T shirt with "Don't stuff yourself, stuff a squirrel for Christmas" as its bright pink slogan.

He glowered at me, and said, "Oh, you made it," in an unfriendly voice. Then he looked up at Feisal and said nothing. They stood staring at each other, glowering, measuring each other up like duellists. I felt gloomily that it was instant dislike on both sides. Feisal's mother had turned him out smartly for the meeting, or else he was neat by nature. He wore beautiful pearl-grey flannels, a red silk shirt, a dark grey corduroy lumber jacket, brand new or just come from the cleaners, and his shoes were beautiful too: Italian, I'd guess —dark red and white with heavy soles and thick white laces.

His face was Arabi's, though: with a dash of something else, just as Bear was like Omar, with some of Sheikhah thrown in. It gave me an odd feeling to see them both standing there, only a couple of hundred metres from where Omar had faced Arabi and asked for paper to write his last letter to his wife and son. Not just an odd feeling, either. Panic. I knew I'd made a dreadful mistake. I looked round, to see if the chauffeur could be persuaded to take me and Bear away out of it, as fast as possible, but the car was already pulling from the kerb in a smooth, purring glide, and my raised arm and involuntary yelp went unanswered. The bloke probably thought the whole assignment was beneath him, anyway —what with Bear's jeans and his slogan shirt.

My yelp broke a kind of spell, though. Feisal unhunched his shoulders and turned to me, saying in a polite, dead voice: "You're Zed, I suppose. The one who wrote the letter. We'd better go to the Park for a bit."

He walked down the steps, giving Bear a long, considering, sideways look. I thought he looked proud altogether, and in that ridiculous gear rather like a Persian prince—large nose, dark eyes, thick dark hair—and not at all like a terrorist's son. Arabi had been untidy and dirty and wild and very much alive.

He began walking fast up the pavement, and Bear and I followed in V formation, like ducklings. Bear said truculently, "You'll fry in that silly gear, can't you leave it?" and Feisal said, "I like it" and just went on walking, only faster. We crossed the road still doing our duckling stunt, just missing a bus, and on through the Park gates, almost steaming along till we hit a patch of green. Feisal stopped there, so suddenly that we almost had a pile-up. He was breathing very fast.

178

"Look here, I don't want to know you any more than you want to know me, right? Or your crawling Lebanese friends and relations." He spoke beautiful English, if you can call what he was saying beautiful; as if he didn't think we were worthy of his Arabic.

"*Right*." Bear's mouth was almost shut, he was breathing hard through his nostrils.

Neither of them seemed to notice me.

"We'll walk round this park till it's teatime, then we'll have tea, then you go home, right?"

"Right."

We began to walk. It began to rain.

They trudged side by side, heads down, hands in their pockets. Feisal jerked his head towards me. "He's your cousin, is he?"

"Yah."

"What does he want? Me to say I'm sorry my father killed yours? Well, I'm not, see? I don't think he did kill him anyway, it was someone else did that, but *if* he did he was right to kill him, that's what I think. Anyway, my father was killed too and I never saw him again, and that got me this stepfather, and if your twit of a father's dead too then serve him right and Allah be praised."

"Here." Bear was standing stockstill, and going poppy red.

"What about here?"

"It's a good place, isn't it? Even ground. It's what I came for—I'm going to slosh you one. I'm going to kill you."

"Right. I'll slosh *you* one, but I'll take my jacket off first."

"And your shoes—they're better than mine."

I began to make a weak protest, but Bear said, "Oh shut up, Zed. What did you think I came for? You can sit on his jacket," and bent down to undo his sandals.

The rain came down faster, as Feisal threw his jacket at me, kicked off his shoes, and rolled the sleeves of his gorgeous silk shirt up above his elbows. He had arms like Arabi's; though they were still small and thin they were packed with muscle.

They went at each other like bantam cocks, some flailing on Bear's part, but Feisal wasn't all that trained, either. In fact, they were pretty evenly matched. Bear had width and more of a swing, but Feisal had the muscle, and an extra inch. They slipped and struggled on the greasy grass, got in a clinch, fell down, got up, and started in again. There was soon mud on Feisal's shirt, and blood on Bear's. Then there was mud on Bear's face, and blood on Feisal's. They looked terrible. Feisal split Bear's lip, and Bear blacked Feisal's eye.

"You sorry yet?" puffed Bear.

"Death or nothing," hissed Feisal, hitting him again. The grass was greasier, and Bear went over backwards, Feisal on top of him. They rolled over and over, pulling at each other's hair, growling insults, pummelling and kicking. Then, just as I was wondering if it wouldn't end till one was dead, the heavens really opened, the hail came hissing down and we were lashed stingingly with hailstones large as mini-marbles, which bounced and rolled and made it impossible to keep our eyes open. The combatants rolled over on their fronts and lay panting.

I said, "Under that tree, quick," and Bear breathed: "No, lightning—" So I said: "Stay here, then?" and spread the jacket so we could all three huddle under it, protecting our heads as best we could. The water streamed down off the jacket like the spray of a waterfall. After a while it lessened, stopped, the sun came out, dozens of little rainbow lights flashed in the trampled grass.

I said resignedly: "Are you going on with it?" and Feisal looked at Bear, and his eyes widened and began to dance, and he said: "Look at your front tooth! It's back to front!"

Bear said, "Is it?" and put up an exploring hand to touch the tooth, and it fell out on the grass.

His round face looked so dismayed that it was funny. Feisal began to laugh—not unpleasantly, he just couldn't help it,

180

and nor could I.

"I'm sorry! I really am—and I'm sorry about your father too. I shouldn't have said all that, I was upset about mine, and everyone being so tolerant and forgiving about it when it hadn't happened to them just made me sick." Feisal was speaking Arabic now, as though Bear was somehow worthy after battle.

And Bear said (sticking to English), "Yes, I see that, but it did happen to your mother and mine, and I haven't forgiven it—though I suppose it's not your fault." He'd spoken in a very adult way, and I thought Feisal was impressed. Then Bear said—looking rather downcast at his tooth— "Shall I throw it away?"

"No. My stepfather's dentist will put it back in for you—he's got a very good dentist. Arab obligation." Feisal looked at me slyly and began to laugh again, and Bear laughed uncertainly, showing a bleeding gap.

That was all, really. They got their things together, and Feisal shook the hail out of his shoes, which were the only smart things left. They looked like a couple of tramps otherwise, even when they'd used handfuls of long wet grass to scrub their mud and blood away. They kept laughing while they did their best to repair each other's damage. "I don't know which of us looks worse," said Bear. "Your shirt's torn right down the back. What will your stepfather say about our fighting?"

Feisal shrugged.

I stood silent, holding my bagged manuscript—an unnecessary referee.

"Why don't you say something, Zed? You've gone all quiet."

"I'm beyond words—though I bet his stepfather won't be."

"You can't tell," said Feisal, rather gloomily. "He'll either be very nice or bloody awful, there's nothing in between. I

181

don't know him very well, even now—but I don't think he's got a between." They began to laugh again.

We walked down Regency Gate looking stranger than when we'd walked up it. We were close to Feisal's home when we saw a tall robed figure waiting in the porch.

Bear began to drag his feet, he clutched at Feisal's arm, breathing into his ear, "Who's that?"

Feisal groaned softly. "The Imam. They never told me he was coming here today—Allah be—" blasphemy was on the tip of his tongue. He wilted slightly.

The front door opened just as we reached the steps. The Imam turned smilingly to wave us in, but his face froze as he took in my companions' state. Feisal hunched his shoulders up to his ears, just as I'd first seen him. All his liveliness disappeared, even his eyes went dull—at least the one which wasn't swollen did.

"It's all right, we're coming in with you," said Bear cheerfully, putting a protective hand on his arm in a way that reminded me of Omar. He looked up into the Imam's face and said confidingly, "We've had an accident, and then we were *practically* hit by lightning, something got my tooth and Feisal's eye. Oh, Zed! Aren't you coming in too? Where are you going?"

"I'm off home—I don't think I'm needed here today. Ring me later." And before anyone could start objecting I began loping down the pavement, clutching my soggy bag of manuscript beneath my arm. The rain had just started again, and I'd only gone a few metres when I heard a horn hooting wildly at me. There, on the opposite side of the road, was the Embassy car, with its chauffeur beckoning to me.

I crossed over to see what he wanted, and he opened the offside door for me to get in, mud and rain and all making a real mess of the beautiful rich-smelling leather.

"Caught by the storm, were you? Want a lift?"

I said, "I don't suppose you're going my way, though?" and

he answered, "That's all right, I'll run you home. It's not my petrol, is it?"

After all, he was really nice. I sat there, nursing my wet manuscript, and wondering if Feisal would end up in big business like Uncle Omar, and Bear as a freedom fighter or terrorist, based on the skills I'd taught him. Anyway, with luck he was on the road to closer connections with his own relations and, it seemed, with Sheikhah's blessing.

As I thought about it, I remembered the heady smells of juniper and pine, the crystal air and alpine flowers of the Christian Mountain—and the rich, underlying smell of Lebanese goat. And I was suddenly very homesick for all these things, the orchards and vineyards and the old people too, my grandfather more than my grandmother, though.

"Here we are," I told the chauffeur, "and thanks very much for the lift."

"Any time," he said cheerfully.

I lingered a moment, admiring the car. "Rather a splendid one for a left-wing government, isn't it?"

"Ah, when you're a bit older, you'll learn—the ones at the top always get the same perks everywhere. That's life, that is. Mind you, there are a few exceptions."

We gave each other the Communist salute, and he drove away.

I reached my own room unseen. Maroun must be out somewhere with Friedl, and I could hear my father and mother arguing in their bedroom. I went along to the kitchen to make myself some coffee, and took it to my room with a good large slab of cake. Zed's metabolism needed pepping up.

Munching, I sat down at my desk, flicking through the MS. I thought there was no further use for it, now Bear didn't seem keen to read it, and MacArthur had a xerox of all he needed for the magazine. So with some relief I tore my masterwork across and across and flung it in my wastepaper basket. Then I sat brooding a little, specially wondering what

Feisal's stepfather had made of Bear's T shirt. It was funny, but after so much drama that was the one thing I wanted to know. I half wished I'd stayed on to tea. Now the evening stretched ahead rather emptily. I wasn't sure if *I'd* gained anything from MacArthur's experiment—except to be told I was a prig and ought to integrate Thomas.

Yes, MacArthur had managed to deflate me, all right—and on top of that there was still George Bastard Shirley's essay waiting for me. Though I speak French well enough, as he'd said, my mother's family's influence—I get tied in knots writing it down. "Well, *Mr.* MacArthur," I said aloud, "this is one side of Thomas-Zed that isn't priggish, just watch me."

I began rapidly roughing out some pages on Marcel P. in English. Just a sort of skeleton or scaffolding on which one of my friends could work. He's a brilliant linguist, and probably knows this Proust's work by heart. A little bribery, that was all it needed, to satisfy old Shirley's standards and remove the least taint of priggishness from Zed.

"Among all the great works of French literature, those of Marcel Proust stand in the first rank, etc, etc..."

It took me quite a time to put up the scaffolding. I ran out of paper near the end, and pulled open the desk drawer to look for more.

The little square photograph of Arabi with Feisal stared up at me—the only one still in my possession. I picked it up, and held it in the palm of my hand, and then propped it on my desk where I could see it, by the red flowers reflected in the window-pane. I looked from the photo to the framed inscription in Arabic hanging above my bed. It had been Omar's favourite saying, and Aunt Sheikhah had given it to me after his death. It was generous of her, because it had always hung above their own bed, wherever they were sleeping.

"Every man has his star, which is born with him and goes out when he dies."

Maybe, I thought: but like all stars their light goes on and on reaching other people, long after they are dead. And I thought that I didn't need red flowers or photographs to make me remember Omar and Arabi, as long as Spring came round.

Also available from Mammoth

Geraldine Kaye

A BREATH OF FRESH AIR

Amy Smith lives in Bristol with her Grandmother as her
mother is often away from home, pursuing her career as a
singer. Amy has never known her father, only that some
mystery surrounds him. However, at school she is
increasingly absorbed by a class project, 'Bristol and the
Slavery Connection' and becomes obsessed by images of the
past which haunt her imagination. One night, during a
thunder storm, Amy glimpses a slave girl outside her window,
and the past takes over.

'Geraldine Kaye recreates the horrors of the slave trade with
enormous sensitivity and also with a clear eye for historical
accuracy. The result is a book which both informs and
moves.'

Children's Book of the Year 1988

Anthony Masters

ALL THE FUN OF THE FAIR

Jim North and his Gallopers – a beautifully painted and carved fairground ride – have an annual date at the Starling Point estate. But this year they have not bargained for the dramatic end of Gerry Kitson's mystery ride, nor the arrival of their new assistant, Leroy. And as Leroy desperately tries to prove himself, the battle to save the Gallopers, not only from bankruptcy but also from vandalism, begins.

ALL THE FUN OF THE FAIR is the first in the *Starling Point* series. Other titles available are:

Anne Holm

I AM DAVID

'David lay quite still in the darkness of the camp, waiting for the signal. "You must get away tonight," the man had told him. "Stay awake so that you're ready just before the guard is changed. When you see me strike a match, the current will be cut off and you can climb over – you'll have half a minute for it, no more."'

Silent and watchful, David, the boy from the camp, tramps across Europe, knowing that at any moment *they* may catch up with him.

This award-winning novel is brilliantly written and deeply moving. It is a story full of hope.

Anne Holm

THE HOSTAGE

Christopher, the son of the Danish Prime Minister, is kidnapped by Mr Møller, one of his father's political opponents. When the operation is taken over by the Red Brigade, who capture Møller's son as well, the kidnapping goes badly wrong, and Chris soon realises that, to stay alive, they must both escape . . .

'I couldn't put it down . . . a story that would hold any reader's attention.'

Times Literary Supplement

'The danger of the situation is described with chilling conviction . . . makes gripping reading.'

The *Guardian*

Gillian Rubinstein

SPACE DEMONS

Space Demons is a computer game with a difference. Imported directly from Japan, it's a prototype destined to lock four unlikely individuals into deadly combat with the sinister forces of its intelligence.

And, as the game draws them into its powerful ambit, Andrew Hayford, Elaine Taylor, Ben Challis and Mario Ferrone are also forced to confront the darker sides of their own natures.

'A wonderful book . . . there's so much to enjoy and reflect on'

Books for Keeps

'The story is compelling . . . and makes ingenious use of science fiction to create a story of human emotions'

Horn Book

Honour Award Australian Book of the Year

Peace Award for Children's Literature

Winner 1988 South Australian Festival Awards

Skymaze is the thrilling sequel to **Space Demons**, also in Mammoth

Catherine Sefton

STARRY NIGHT
FRANKIE'S STORY
BEAT OF THE DRUM

Catherine Sefton's moving trilogy shows how the political
and social situation in Northern Ireland affects young people
on both sides of the divide at critical moments in their lives.
Each book considers different viewpoints: the disturbing
truth behind the crisis in Kathleen's family (STARRY
NIGHT); the trouble encountered by the unconventional
Catholic, Frankie, who has a Protestant boyfriend
(FRANKIE'S STORY); and finally a look at loyalist
Protestants through the eyes of young, crippled, Brian Hanna
(BEAT OF THE DRUM).

A Selected List of Fiction from Mammoth

While every effort is made to keep prices low, it is sometimes necessary to increase prices at short notice. Mammoth Books reserves the right to show new retail prices on covers which may differ from those previously advertised in the text or elsewhere.

The prices shown below were correct at the time of going to press.

☐	416 13972 8	**Why the Whales Came**	Michael Morpurgo	£2.50
☐	7497 0034 3	**My Friend Walter**	Michael Morpurgo	£2.50
☐	7497 0035 1	**The Animals of Farthing Wood**	Colin Dann	£2.99
☐	7497 0136 6	**I Am David**	Anne Holm	£2.50
☐	7497 0139 0	**Snow Spider**	Jenny Nimmo	£2.50
☐	7497 0140 4	**Emlyn's Moon**	Jenny Nimmo	£2.25
☐	7497 0344 X	**The Haunting**	Margaret Mahy	£2.25
☐	416 96850 3	**Catalogue of the Universe**	Margaret Mahy	£1.95
☐	7497 0051 3	**My Friend Flicka**	Mary O'Hara	£2.99
☐	7497 0079 3	**Thunderhead**	Mary O'Hara	£2.99
☐	7497 0219 2	**Green Grass of Wyoming**	Mary O'Hara	£2.99
☐	416 13722 9	**Rival Games**	Michael Hardcastle	£1.99
☐	416 13212 X	**Mascot**	Michael Hardcastle	£1.99
☐	7497 0126 9	**Half a Team**	Michael Hardcastle	£1.99
☐	416 08812 0	**The Whipping Boy**	Sid Fleischman	£1.99
☐	7497 0033 5	**The Lives of Christopher Chant**	Diana Wynne-Jones	£2.50
☐	7497 0164 1	**A Visit to Folly Castle**	Nina Beachcroft	£2.25

All these books are available at your bookshop or newsagent, or can be ordered direct from the publisher. Just tick the titles you want and fill in the form below.

Mandarin Paperbacks, Cash Sales Department, PO Box 11, Falmouth, Cornwall TR10 9EN.

Please send cheque or postal order, no currency, for purchase price quoted and allow the following for postage and packing:

UK	80p for the first book, 20p for each additional book ordered to a maximum charge of £2.00.
BFPO	80p for the first book, 20p for each additional book.
Overseas including Eire	£1.50 for the first book, £1.00 for the second and 30p for each additional book thereafter.

NAME (Block letters) ....

ADDRESS ....

....

....